THE DRAGON IN THE LIBRARY

LOUIE STOWELL

illustrated by
DAVIDE ORTU

Walker Books

Text copyright © 2019 by Louie Stowell
Illustrations copyright © 2019 by Davide Ortu

First US edition 2021
First published by Nosy Crow (UK) 2019

Library of Congress Catalog Card Number pending
ISBN 978-1-5362-1493-2 (hardcover)
ISBN 978-1-5362-1960-9 (paperback)

20 21 22 23 24 25 LBM 10 9 8 7 6 5 4 3 2 1

Printed in Melrose Park, IL, USA

This book was typeset in Chaparral Pro.
The illustrations were created digitally.

Walker Books US
a division of
Candlewick Press
99 Dover Street
Somerville, Massachusetts 02144

www.walkerbooksus.com

To Karen
LS

For my beloved friend Anna,
the strongest woman I know
DO

CHAPTER 1

THE HUNT FOR DANNY FANDANGO

Do you seriously want to spend the first day of summer vacation with a bunch of dead people?" Josh asked. He was a tall, skinny boy with brown skin and tight curls. If you had to pick one word to describe him, he'd be very disappointed in you, because Josh believed that a wide vocabulary was very important.

"They're buried!" Kit said. "It's not like they're zombies. It's just a cemetery. And it's so overgrown it's basically a park." Kit was stocky, pale, and red-haired. If you had to pick one word to describe her, it would probably be *muddy*.

"A park full of dead bodies," Josh said with a shudder. "I don't care if they're buried. I'll still know they're there."

It was the beginning of summer vacation, and Kit and her friends were sitting on Kit's bedroom floor, arguing about what to do that day.

"Let's go to the library instead," said Alita. "There are absolutely no dead bodies anywhere in the library."

"Yet," said Kit darkly. "What if I die of boredom?"

Alita was about half Kit's size in every direction. Her eyes were dark, her skin was brown, and her thick black hair was divided into two perfect braids. If you had to pick one word to describe her, it would probably be *intense*. Her eyes looked as if they could bore through solid concrete.

Josh sat upright, making excited gestures with his long, skinny arms. "You won't die of boredom. There are so many books at the library!"

"But I don't like books," protested Kit. "They have words in them."

"*You* don't have to read them," said Alita. "But I need to get a book. Urgently. It's basically a matter of life and death."

"But it's so . . . *bluuuuurrrgh* in the library," complained Kit.

"Pleeeease," Alita went on. "I need the new Danny Fandango, and if we're not quick, all the copies will be gone. I've been waiting a *year* to find out what happens next."

It was a beautiful sunny day. Kit, Josh, and Alita were allowed to walk anywhere within a mile as long as they stuck together. Freedom was theirs. But for some baffling reason, Kit's friends wanted to go somewhere you had to be quiet and behave. Sometimes her friends made no sense. And not just when they used really long words.

"If we go to the cemetery instead of the library, we can climb trees!" said Kit. This, she felt, was a powerful argument.

"Or, to put it another way," said Josh, "if we go to the cemetery, we'll *have* to climb trees. And get mud on ourselves." He gestured down at his pristine sneakers. Kit didn't understand how it was possible for shoes to stay that clean.

"And maybe, if we climb trees," Josh went on, "we'll fall from a great height and die."

"We won't die," said Kit.

"OK, we'll be maimed, then," said Josh. "I don't want to be maimed. I want to read Danny Fandango."

"Come on, Kit. We can go to the cemetery afterward. We *promise*," said Alita. She gave a pleading look, opening her dark eyes wide and fluttering her long eyelashes. Kit knew that trick—Alita was the baby of her family, and she always got her own way.

"Yes, we promise. I swear on my signed copy of *Danny Fandango and the Cauldron of Poison*," said Josh.

This was a serious oath, Kit knew. Josh kept the book in his bedroom in a glass case like it was a museum exhibit. Kit wouldn't be surprised if he had set up lasers and alarms all around it.

"Come on, Kit," repeated Alita, who was almost as big a Danny Fandango fan as Josh, although not as into lasers. She was more likely to have trained her dog to guard her copy. Alita's dog scared most people. It was big enough to ride like a horse. But Alita treated it like a cute little kitten and had named it Fluffy. She'd insisted they adopt it from a dog shelter. Kit wondered how the dog shelter people had stopped it from eating all the other dogs.

"I suppose we *could* go to the library *first* . . . " said Kit, thinking longingly about the overgrown cemetery with its spooky stone angels and matted undergrowth full of cool insects and—one blissful day—a rat. "But just quickly, all right?"

"Quick as Danny Fandango casting a Lightning Spell!" said Josh.

"Quick as Lara Fandango casting an even faster one!" said Alita.

Kit hadn't read any of the Danny Fandango books because reading required sitting still, and sitting still was against everything she stood for. But from what Kit had picked up from her friends, Lara was Danny's sister, and she was better at magic, but he was the Chosen One so got to do all the fun stuff.

That sounded familiar. Kit's older brother and sister always got to do the fun stuff. Kit's Perfect Older Sister was Perfect in All Ways, according to her parents. Kit's Wicked Older Brother was a Bad Boy and therefore required a lot of shouting and attention, and when he did even the slightest thing right, he got presents. Kit's younger sister was only a toddler, and her job was to be Adorable and Covered in Jam. And her baby brother had a tiny scrunched-up face, cried a lot, and was Precious and Good Enough to Eat.

Kit was . . . nothing in particular. She was average. Not incredibly smart, but not unintelligent. Not especially sporty, but not unable to catch, either. When people were picking teams, she was usually picked second or third. Never first. Never last.

The only non-average thing about her was her size. Growing out of her sister's hand-me-downs at an unnatural rate was her most remarkable skill, according to her parents. She was in the last year of elementary school now, but she had grown out of all of Perfect Older Sister's school uniforms, so they'd had to buy a new one in the spring. That had led to a lot of tutting, but Kit didn't see how it was her fault. She wasn't growing on purpose. It just happened.

"Let's get this over with, then," said Kit. "We're

going out!" she called as she passed her parents and her two younger siblings in the living room.

Alita looked shocked by Kit's dad, who was holding Toddler upside down, bouncing her up and down like a sack of potatoes.

"Who's a bouncy bouncy bouncy?" he was saying.

Alita was too polite to say so, but Kit knew she was thinking that nothing like that would happen in her house, where the adults were dignified and people were usually the right way up, however old they were.

"Hello, Mr. Spencer! Mrs. Spencer!" said Josh.

"Hello, Josh! Hello, Alita! See you later! Don't get muddy, Kit!" said her mom, wiping a splotch of baby food out of her auburn hair. She glanced at Kit. "Mudd*ier*." Then, to Kit's dad, "The baby's spit up again. Can you pass me a wet wipe?"

Kit sometimes wondered if her parents might pay more attention to her if *she* had vomit and snot streaming out of her all the time.

The Chatsworth Library was a boring-looking concrete building with automatic doors that didn't work right, so you had to approach them and then retreat a couple of times before you could get through.

They'd never been to this library before, but the one that Josh and Alita usually went to had closed down a few months before. This one looked like any other library, though. Inside, the walls were covered in posters about getting flu vaccinations and rules about when you could use the computers. There was a little play area with toys for small children. Kit wished they had one of those for kids her age. Maybe a multicolored ball pit that you could dive into. She'd be at the library every day if they did.

"The new Danny Fandangos will be over here," said Josh, charging toward the children's section.

"OK, get it quickly, and then we can go to the cemetery," said Kit. The silence in the library was creepy. It made her want to shout really, really loudly.

At that moment, she caught the eye of a librarian with a long white beard who put a finger to his lips, as if he *knew* she was going to make a noise.

Kit sighed and strolled over to her friends. They were staring at a display of books. Or rather, at an *empty* space in the center of it.

"It's already gone!" said Alita. "*Danny Fandango and the Crown of Bones* is gone!"

"We're too late!" said Josh.

"This is the worst thing that has ever happened," said Alita. "Including when Lara Fandango's pet fox lost a leg in book two."

They both turned to Kit. "This is your fault!" said Josh.

"What? We only got here five minutes after opening time!" said Kit.

"Exactly," said Josh. "I bet people were lining up before the library opened. Probably overnight. I wish we were older so we were allowed to line up overnight."

Kit could think of a million reasons why being older would be fun, but none of them involved lining up.

"Can I help?" said a voice from behind them.

Kit turned to see a tall, dark-skinned Black woman with her hair in long locs. Her face was open and warm, with a wide nose and a full, perfectly lipsticked mouth. Her long nails were painted with squiggly, shimmering patterns.

The woman was wearing a name tag that said FAITH BRAITHWAITE, HEAD LIBRARIAN.

"What are you looking for?" Faith the Head Librarian asked with a bright smile.

"The new Danny Fandango!" said Alita and Josh in unison.

Faith put her hands to her heart in a gesture of shock. "*Danny Fandango and the Crown of Bones?* Oh, no. Not to be funny, but you've got to get up earlier in the morning if you want to get a copy of that the day it arrives. People were lined up when the library opened. All the copies will be out for at least a week now."

Alita and Josh looked like puppies who'd just been kicked.

"A week? That's . . . so long," said Alita. Her eyes filled with tears.

"A week?" asked Josh, biting his lip. "But *Crown of Bones* is only seven hundred pages long. Do people really read that slowly?"

"It's not a race. No one gets medals for reading quickly," said Faith.

Josh looked extra sad at that.

"Cheer up, though," Faith went on. "There are other books. That's the point of this place. Read these instead."

She produced two identical books from behind her back, as though she'd been holding on to them the whole time. Except that was impossible, Kit thought. Her hands had been empty moments before.

The books said *The Wizard of Earthsea* on their covers.

Josh and Alita perked up ever so slightly.

"Wizards?" said Josh, taking his copy. "Excellent!"

The librarian turned to Kit. "What about you?"

"Oh, I don't need a book." Kit pointed to her friends. "I'm just here for them. We're going to the cemetery now." But Josh and Alita had already scuttled off to a reading corner with their books.

"Never mind them," said Faith. "What kind of story would you like?"

"I don't really like stories," said Kit.

"How do you think the stories feel, with you talking about them like that?" asked Faith.

"Sorry," mumbled Kit. Then she blinked. "Wait, stories don't have feelings."

"Don't they?" Faith raised an eyebrow. "Are you saying you're the expert on stories around here?" She tapped her Head Librarian badge. "Tell that to the badge."

"I'm not, but—"

"I'll stop you there," Faith said, holding up a

finger. "You don't like stories, you say? Well, not all books are stories. Follow me." She strode through the aisles, locs bouncing, with Kit trotting behind her to catch up.

Faith stopped suddenly in front of a shelf marked NONFICTION. Kit bumped into her, then fell over her own feet with a *thump*. Faith looked down at her curiously.

"What do you like doing?" she asked as Kit scrambled upright. The librarian flung out her arms in a wide gesture, taking in the entire library—or possibly the entire world. "What's your favorite thing to do? I want to pick the perfect book. Be specific. Be honest."

Kit thought about it. "I like . . . being outside. Burning stuff. Exploring. Danger." She looked down at herself and, being honest, added, "Mud."

"Hmmmm," said Faith. She turned to the shelf behind her and pulled out a book with a picture of a burning town on the front called *The Great Fire of London*.

"Here, try this. There's plenty of fire, obviously,

and it's about the seventeenth century, so that takes care of the mud. Everyone was muddy then. Even rich people."

Kit took the book, feeling skeptical. She thought she'd rather build a fire than read about one.

"If you don't like it, I'll give you your money back," said Faith.

"But books are free at the library," objected Kit.

"Well, isn't that great!" Faith grinned. "Later!" She gave Kit a little nod, then strode away.

Before Kit had a chance to open the book, she heard a loud click from behind the nearest shelf, making her jump.

She went to investigate. Behind the shelf was a cabinet full of books behind sliding glass doors. There was a padlock on one of the doors. It was unlocked.

She found herself sliding the glass door back. The first book that caught her eye was called *Dangerous Animals*. It was very old and very dusty. She couldn't say why, but she reached for it.

"Ow!" she yelped. The book had given Kit a tiny

electric shock. *Books can tell I don't like them,* she thought glumly. *It's like how dogs can smell fear.*

She looked at the book more closely and flipped it open. On the first page was a picture of a huge snake with a label that read *Black Mamba,* along with facts about how big it was, how fast, how poisonous . . . *OK,* thought Kit. This book was more interesting than it looked.

Kit could've sworn she heard a hiss. She peered more closely at the image of the snake. Its beady black eyes seemed huge.

She heard the hiss again.

But Kit wasn't standing in the library anymore. She was in a rocky desert. In front of her, the mamba rose up on its tail, swishing from side to side, hissing.

It's about to strike, she thought. She wanted to scream. She wanted to run. But she'd just read that the mamba was too fast to outrun. She stood, helpless, waiting to feel the venomous creature's teeth sink into her . . .

There was a rushing sound in her ears, and she found herself in the library again.

No. Not *the* library. *A* library. The shelves were taller. And outside the window, there was a tree.

There was a flash.

She was back in the desert. The snake was mid-strike.

Then she felt someone take her hand. She heard a muttered word. The snake's hiss was in her ears.

Then it wasn't.

CHAPTER 2

A SUNLIT GARDEN

Kit blinked. She was back in the library, and Faith the librarian was by her side, holding the closed book of dangerous animals in one hand and Kit's hand in the other.

"Well, *that* shouldn't have happened," said Faith, letting go of her. She looked down at the book, then over at Kit, shaking her head.

"What *did* happen?" Kit glared at the book, in case it got any more funny ideas. "There was a *snake,* and I was in a book, and then I was in a different library, and . . ." Kit couldn't finish. This all made as much sense to her as a math lesson in another language.

"Hmmm," was all Faith said. And then, "Was that the first time something like that has happened to you?"

Kit stared at her in disbelief. "Of *course* it's the first time. Definitely. I'd remember."

"All right, all right," said Faith. She put a finger to her lips. "Inside voice. This is a library, remember?"

"Are you sure?" asked Kit. "Libraries don't usually have so many snakes!"

"Depends on the library," said Faith. She ran her finger along a row of books behind the glass, sliding the doors farther out of the way. "Let's try something less dangerous." She picked out a volume called *Gardens of the World*.

It looked like the sort of book Kit's dad would like.

"Try reading this one to yourself," suggested Faith. "I'll prop it up for you on this shelf here . . . just in case that wasn't a fluke last time." She opened the book to one of the first pages, placing it carefully on a shelf at Kit's eye level.

"OK . . . " Kit didn't know what was going on. She wasn't sure she liked it. But on the other hand, she wasn't sure she *didn't* like it, either. It was definitely not boring. The library was no longer a place of dust and quiet. It was *weird*. And she liked weird.

Kit began to read. "In climates with little sunlight, why not try a rock garden? A birdfeeder will attract wildlife. And selecting shrubs that bees find appealing will—"

There was a low hum. Without fanfare—not even a tiny toot on a trumpet—Kit was suddenly in a garden. Birds flapped around a stuffed birdfeeder. There were rocks and little shrubs all around her. Bees buzzed between the strongly scented bushes.

She glanced to one side. Faith was standing there, arms folded.

"Well, well, well," she said. "I'm impressed. This really shouldn't be possible."

"Standing inside a book? No, it shouldn't," said Kit. "You *read* books. You don't *stand* in them."

She turned her head, then spun all around. "Is this some kind of hologram?"

Faith shook her head. "Nope." She paused, turning her face up toward t. sun, and closed her eyes to bathe in the light. "It magic, obviously."

Kit's heart skipped like a stone on water. She felt tingles all over her skin.

"This is a magical book?" Kit looked around in wonder. She sniffed the air cautiously. She could smell flowers and herbs and a little rain. It smelled so real.

Faith gave a half nod, half shake of her head. "It's partly the book that's magical, yes. But it's partly you."

"Sorry?" Kit blinked. "What do you mean, me? What am I?"

"You're a wizard."

Kit blinked again. "I'm a *what*?"

"A wizard." Faith raised a finger and wagged it. "But you

shouldn't be a wizard. It's not supposed to happen."

Faith pursed her lips. This annoyed Kit.

"Is it because I'm a girl? Can't girls be wizards?"

Faith gave her a look. "No," she said patiently. "It's not because you're a girl. It's because you're a child."

Kit stroked her chin. "So to be a wizard, do I need to be old enough to have a long white beard?"

"Do *I* have a long white beard?" Faith pointed to her own very smooth brown chin.

Kit gasped. "*You're* a wizard? I thought you were a librarian."

"Are you saying a person can't be more than one thing?" asked Faith.

"No," said Kit. "I just . . . "

"You can *just* later. We should be getting back." Faith looked around the garden and licked her lips a little nervously. "It's not good to stay in one place for too long in here. You can . . . lose yourself."

"How *do* we get back?" Kit looked around. The garden seemed to stretch forever in every direction. She couldn't see a way out.

Faith snapped her fingers, striking purple sparks as she did so. "We do a spell, of course."

It seemed obvious when Faith said it. Wizards do spells. It's what makes you a wizard.

"So how do I do a spell to get us home, then?" asked Kit.

Faith looked horrified. "Oh, no, you're not going to do a spell. You haven't had any training."

Kit felt secretly relieved.

Faith breathed gently, in and out, and gestured with her left hand—a little slice of the air, hardly a movement at all. And then, after another breath, she said, *"Hus!"*

Without a warning, without a flash, without a sound, they were back in the library. Faith glanced around. There was no one nearby.

"Come on," said Faith. "Let's go and talk somewhere." And she led Kit to a little office on the other side of the library. It was shabby and didn't appear to be used very often, with just a plastic chair and a desk with a couple of torn books resting on it. Faith placed the garden book on the table. "I'll shelve that in a moment. First, what would you like to know?"

Kit's brain was teeming with questions, like a pond full of hyperactive tadpoles.

"Where *were* we? How did all that"—she waved at the book—"work?"

"We were inside the book," said Faith. "But we were also on our way to another library—it could be any library in the world, depending on the exit spell you say when you reach the end of the book. We use certain books—we call them portal books—to travel between libraries. Any book can take you to any library with another copy of the same book. You just walk all the way through the book, then say the right spell to take you to the library you want. The landscape you see around you as you walk depends on the book, and also on the person reading it. That garden looks a little different when I read it. And it looks different every time you read it, depending on your mood or what else you've read recently. But the short answer is, we were inside a book."

"So we were standing on a page? It looked like grass," said Kit.

"It's not quite that simple," said Faith. "We weren't inside the book in that way. It's more like . . . the magical space in the world created *by* the book—by the act of you reading it. This world doesn't take up any physical space. You could think of it as the book's soul, if that helps."

Kit wasn't sure that it did. But she had another, more important question, hopefully one with a simpler answer. "And . . . I'm a wizard?"

"Yes!" said Faith. "The youngest wizard in the world." She thought about this for a moment. "Probably."

"Oh," said Kit. "Wow."

Not only was she a wizard, she was some kind of magical child prodigy. This was *huge*.

"Normally," Faith went on, "a wizard's powers don't kick in until they're eighteen." She looked at Kit in puzzlement. "Things really aren't set up for child wizards." But then she got a glint in her eye. "We'll just have to improvise."

"Wow!" said Kit. "I can do *magic*!" She had a thought. "I can't wait to tell the others! They *love* magic. They're going to scream when they find out it's real!"

"Oh, no, no, no!" Faith waved her hands at Kit. "You can't do that. You can't tell them anything. You can't tell anyone."

"Why not?" Kit's heart sank.

"Because of what happens whenever the public finds out about magic. It's happened before, you see."

"When?" Kit definitely hadn't heard about magic being real before. Except the kind with playing cards and rabbits in hats.

"Have you heard of witch burnings?" said Faith. "That's what happened last time someone found out about magic in Europe. I mean, technically they were wizard burnings. Witches don't exist. But when you're being burned at the stake, you don't really care about whether they're getting your job title correct."

"But I only want to tell Josh and Alita, not

the whole world," objected Kit. "Josh and Alita wouldn't burn wizards. Josh is afraid of fire, and Alita is too nice to burn an ant with a magnifying glass."

Faith sighed. "It's not about what *they'd* do. It's other people I'm worried about."

Kit sniffed. Grown-ups were always warning her about risks, but nothing ever happened. *Don't climb that tree, Kit; it's too risky—you might fall . . . Kit, don't tip back on your chair; it's too risky—you might crack your head . . . Kit, don't stick that fork in that electric socket; you might . . .*

OK, those last two *had* led to trips to the hospital. But still. *Most of the time* things didn't end as doomily and gloomily as adults expected.

Kit folded her arms. "They're my best friends. You can't stop me from telling them."

Faith folded her arms, too. Her eyes were hard. "No. I can't stop you. But if you do tell them, I'll have to cast a spell to wipe their minds. And I *hate* doing that."

There was a scuffle at the door, and all of a

sudden, Alita and Josh burst in, Josh in front and Alita hissing at him to get back.

"Please don't wipe our brains!" said Josh. "I need my brain! It's my best feature! It's where I keep my ideas!"

"Sorry to barge in so rudely," said Alita. "What Josh was trying to say was, please don't do a spell to make us forget. We won't tell anyone—we promise."

"We're good at keeping secrets about Kit," said Josh. "We *still* haven't told Kit's mom that Kit broke the toilet last week."

Faith gave a big sigh and closed the door behind them after checking that no one else was close by. "Well, this is a new career high for me," she muttered. She looked at Josh and Alita for a long time.

"So," she said at last, "I take it you overheard what we were talking about? Although, when I say 'overheard,' I mean 'listened in on something that is definitely *not* your business.'"

Josh and Alita nodded sheepishly.

"We knew it was wrong," said Alita. "But"—she

looked up at Faith with her big intense eyes—"so is wiping people's brains."

Faith raised an eyebrow.

"I took notes," said Josh, holding up a small notepad and pencil that he carried around with him everywhere.

"So," Josh went on, "even if you wipe our minds, there'll still be a record."

"And we didn't *just* overhear," added Alita. "We saw you appear out of that book, from nowhere!" She pointed at the garden book.

Faith rubbed her eyes and sighed. "Well, that's not good. It's even harder to wipe someone's mind when they've seen things with their own eyes. More dangerous." A light seemed to crackle around her. She lifted her hands, palms out toward Josh and Alita. "But can I really leave the fate of all wizards in the hands of a couple of eavesdropping children?"

"No!" gasped Kit. "Don't!"

Josh and Alita closed their eyes, bracing to have their minds wiped.

CHAPTER 3

THE STACKS

No," said Faith at last. "I won't do it."

All three children let out enormous sighs of relief.

"*Phew!*" said Alita.

"Double *phew!*" said Kit.

"Thanks. But *why* won't you do it?" asked Josh. "What changed your mind?" He pulled out his notebook again. "I'd really like to understand what makes wizards tick. Also, I have some further questions."

"Josh!" hissed Alita.

But Faith was smiling. "I don't care what the Wizards' Council will say. I can't risk it. You've seen so much that I'd have to take more of your memories than is safe. So I won't do it. I just hope I'm doing the right thing."

"Well, I definitely think you're doing the right thing," said Josh. "But perhaps you could tell us more about this Wizards' Council. It sounds very—Ow!"

Josh was silenced by a sharp elbow to the gut from Alita.

Faith looked carefully at Josh and Alita. "I won't make you forget. But I need you to swear not to reveal the secrets of the library."

"We swear!" they said together.

"And I swear, too," said Kit. "Just in case that helps."

"Good enough for me," said Faith, breaking into a smile. "And now you might as well see the rest of the library. And have something to drink. And maybe to eat?"

All three children nodded enthusiastically.

Faith led them through the bookshelves as Josh and Alita fired questions at her.

"Which books are magical, apart from the

garden book you went into?" asked Alita. "How can you tell if a book is magical?"

"How do you know if you're a wizard?" asked Josh. "Am I a wizard?"

Faith paused for a second. She passed both hands back and forth through the air, across Josh and Alita, saying, *"Prak at Karin . . ."* She paused, then shook her head. "No. Not yet, anyway. Nor you, Alita," she added, and carried on through the bookshelves.

"Not yet? Do you mean we might be later?" asked Alita. "I don't know what my mom would think about that." Then, after seeing Faith's stern look, she added, "Not that I'd tell her, obviously. But I'm pretty sure she wouldn't approve. I don't think she'd think being a wizard is a real job."

"Hey!" said Faith.

Alita gave an embarrassed cough. "Uh . . . sorry."

Faith flashed a smile. "It's OK. I don't think my mom would approve either, if she knew."

"Your mom doesn't know you're a wizard?" Alita's eyes opened very wide. "What does she think you are?"

"A librarian," said Faith. "Which, technically, is *not* a lie."

Faith led them down a narrow alley between two shelves in a dusty corner of the library to a door marked THE STACKS, with another sign below it saying STAFF ONLY.

Faith glanced behind her to check that there was no one else around. She beckoned them closer, then reached out to touch a book, pulling it half off the shelf and whispering something that sounded like *"labba."*

A slight glow emerged from between her fingers, and then the whole shelf slid aside without a sound, revealing a doorway.

Josh let out an excited "Wow!" but Faith put a finger to her lips and whispered, "Let's not tell the whole library about the *secret* passage, eh?"

"Sorry," Josh whispered.

Inside the doorway, it was completely dark.

"Go on ahead," said Faith. "Don't be scared. It's perfectly safe. Very few people have died down here."

Kit wasn't
sure that Faith's
idea of "perfectly safe"
was the same as most people's.

The wizard librarian ushered the children through the opening ahead of her. When they were all through, the shelf slid silently back into place. They were in total darkness.

"*Ina,*" Faith whispered, touching Kit on the forehead.

A ball of light appeared, lighting up the corridor ahead.

Kit could now see that the passage sloped downward. The walls were lined with books.

Kit strode ahead along the corridor, eager to see

what was
down there. The
others trotted behind her, with
Josh at Faith's side, asking questions.

"What spell was that, that made the light?"

"A light spell. A spell of elemental magic."

"What's elemental magic? Can Kit do elemental magic?"

"Josh, has anyone ever told you that you ask a lot of questions?" asked Faith.

"Most adults, most of the time," said Josh.

It was true. In class, Josh had his hand up so often that he once had to go to the school nurse with a sprained shoulder.

"Where are we now?" he asked, adding to the pile of questions.

"This is where we keep the books we don't want the general public to get its hands on," said Faith.

"Because they're expensive?" asked Kit.

"Because they're dangerous," said Faith. She gestured around at the book-lined walls. "These books have power, even if you're not a wizard."

Now that Faith mentioned it, Kit could feel something coming from the books. She felt drawn to them, as she had with the garden book and the snake book in the glass case. They seemed to be . . . humming.

"These books could change you in ways you can't even imagine," Faith said.

"I can imagine a lot of things," said Josh.

"Then double it," said Faith. "And add a part where your head gets turned into a marshmallow and your arms become tentacles."

The children stayed as close to the middle of the corridor as they could after that.

The ground was getting soft beneath their feet. Sort of squishy and springy. The light from the spell began to fade, and a new light grew around them.

Kit couldn't say when the walls of books became a forest surrounding them.

The wood was dense with trees covered in carvings, as though thousands of people had written their names there over the years.

"Where are we?" breathed Kit.

"In the stacks," said Faith.

"But where are all the books?" asked Josh.

"Still there. Look," said Faith. She beckoned them closer to the nearest tree. Soft green light illuminated the bark. It was covered in writing—but not in English. The leaves of the tree were green, but when Kit looked at them for a

moment, she real-
ized they weren't leaves,
exactly—they were pale-green,
leaf-shaped pages, written all over
in darker ink.

Faith took one of the leaf-pages between
her finger and thumb, ever so gently. "Books
come from trees," she said, releasing the leaf
just as gently. "Give them enough magic,
and they'll come back to life. But they don't
ever stop being books."

Josh was peering closely at some of the
writing on one of the leaves. *"Hwa . . . hwaa
at . . . ne . . . ouv . . . "*

"Don't read it out loud, for Smaug's sake!"
Faith clapped her hand over Josh's mouth.
"That's a spell! If anyone reads that out loud,
bad things happen. Remember what I *just*
said about marshmallows and tentacles?"

"OK, but . . . what you're saying is that
anyone can do magic if they find the right
magical book?" asked Josh hopefully.

"No. What I'm saying is, no reading spells from books or trees out loud. Any of you." Faith stood between them and the tree. "And especially not you," she said to Kit.

"You don't have to warn me not to read," said Kit.

"Oh, really." Faith laughed. "And there I was thinking you were such a book-worm." She folded her arms in front of her. "But I'm afraid there will be plenty of reading for you. Just not spells yet."

Alita was standing by a tree, stroking one of its thick branches. "Oooh, the moss! It's so soft! And warm!"

Faith looked confused.

Just then, the branch Alita was stroking moved. A creature rose up into the air with a flurry of wings and a *WHOOSH!*

A ball of fire the size of an

orange shot through the air. Alita shrieked, leaping back.

"*Agua!*" said Faith, waving her hand in a little rainbow-shaped arc. A jet of water leaped through the air, as though someone had turned on an invisible tap.

The creature let out a whimper and fluttered to the ground, shaking water out of its large, floppy ears.

It was about the size of a large puppy, with big brown eyes, a furry red muzzle and coat, and red wings. Its belly was covered in green scales. It was adorable. But what *was* it?

Dogon!" scolded Faith. "No breathing fire at guests!"

"Gruff!" said the creature, looking up at Faith in annoyance. "Rrrrr!" It shook its floppy ears again, sending water flying everywhere.

"I just can't seem to get Dogon to behave," said Faith. "He's so naughty! Are you all right, Alita?"

"Fine! Just a bit damp. What *is* he?" asked Alita, coming closer to the thing. He nuzzled into her outstretched hand, making a purring sound.

"He's a dogon. *The* Dogon, in fact. The one and

only half dog, half dragon," said Faith. "He lives here. He's lived here for years, as long as I've been here. He doesn't usually come over and say hello. Perhaps he likes children."

"But how can he have been here for years? He's just a puppy," said Alita, continuing to stroke the dogon. The creature arched his back and wagged his tail happily.

"Magical creatures don't age in the same way that others do," said Faith.

"So if Dogon is half dragon, half dog, does that mean there are dragons, too?" asked Josh.

Faith just smiled. "Why don't we have something to eat?"

"Magic food?" asked Alita hopefully.

"Definitely not," said Faith. "Never eat magical food if you can help it. Unless you enjoy being turned into something slimy. Oh, and before I forget . . . *Sec!*"

"I'm dry!" gasped Alita. She patted her arms and grinned. "Magic!"

The wood continued onward for a while, and the children looked around at the gnarled, carved trees. Dogon flapped behind them, staying close to Alita. Kit sniffed the air. It didn't smell entirely like a forest. There was a musty, dry smell, too.

Like books.

The book forest gradually thinned out, and eventually they reached a clearing with one very large tree in the middle. Faith placed a palm on the trunk and said something that sounded like *"Hoogah!"*

A door slid back, disappearing with a ripple of bark. Inside, Kit caught a glimpse of a cheerful, messy room.

Faith led them inside the tree, and the door shut behind them. On the inside, it looked like an ordinary wooden door, not a tree at all. The walls were covered in wallpaper decorated with stars.

The room had some very scruffy armchairs, a desk with messy piles of paper, a small fridge, some cupboards, and a sink with a kettle next to it, along with tea bags, spoons, and a cookie tin. There was a shelf of what Kit thought must be spell

books—they were certainly very old, with gold on the spines and writing in languages that Kit didn't understand.

"Welcome to the common room," said Faith. "It's where we take our breaks."

"Couldn't you do a tidying spell?" suggested Josh.

"What do you mean?" said Faith. "Everything's exactly where I want it."

Josh looked dubious.

Faith gestured them toward the armchairs. Kit sat in a huge, squishy-looking one. She felt something lumpy behind her and patted around until she pulled out a ring with a gemstone in it.

"Ah, I'd better take that," said Faith. She got up and dug around in a drawer in the desk.

"What is it?" asked Kit, standing up.

"Ring of great power. Belonged to an evil wizard. You probably shouldn't touch it. Evil wizardry can be contagious." She reached out with a pair of tongs and plucked the ring out of Kit's hand, dropping it into an envelope and putting it into her pocket.

"I thought you said everything was where you wanted it?" said Josh.

Faith gave him a look. "Perhaps it was there so that I could teach you the importance of not touching magical rings?" Josh shrank back a little.

"Would anyone like some lemonade?" asked Faith, bustling to the kitchen sink in the corner and taking a jug from the cupboard. "Ginger cake? They're homemade."

Everyone raised their hands. Discovering that magic existed was hungry and thirsty work.

Faith took some lemons and limes from a bowl and started to squeeze them into the jug. She opened a tin with a moist-looking cake inside. A warm, gingery smell wafted through the air as she put it on a plate, then went back to squeezing the fruit. "So. Does anyone have any questions?"

"You said the light spell you did was elemental magic," said Josh. "What other types of magic are there?" He took out his notebook, pen poised.

As Faith juiced and talked, Josh scribbled.

There are seven
kinds of magic spells.

1. **Elemental**: Spells based
on water, fire, earth, or
air. For example, using
magic to create a giant
fireball. (Faith told Kit
not to look quite so
excited about that.)

2. **Physical**: Moving
objects or people around
using magic. For example,
making things float in
the air.

3. **Scrying**: Magic
that helps you find
out information.
Maybe I could
get Kit to use

a scrying spell to find out where I left my favorite Star Wars socks?

4. **Illusion**: Magic that makes things look like other things.

5. **Transformation**: Magic that makes things literally turn into other things.

"So," interrupted Kit, "I could turn into a bear or a lion or whatever if I wanted to?"

"One day," said Faith. "Although I'd recommend starting with slightly less dangerous animals. Maybe a ferret? Or a wood louse?"

"No fun," huffed Kit.

"What type of magic does Dogon have?" asked Alita. The creature was licking Alita's hand, and she batted him away. "No, Dogon."

Dogon stopped licking, his pink tongue sticking out goofily from between his pointed teeth.

"Wild magic," said Faith. "That's the most dangerous kind."

"Should Alita be petting him?" asked Kit, suddenly worried.

"Awww, Dogon's not dangerous. Look at him. He's so fluffy!" said Alita.

"Alita's right," said Faith. "Dogon only has a little wild magic. But if it's found in large quantities, unless it's tamed, it can cause all kinds of problems."

6. **Wild**: Dangerous. Faith says that ALL magic comes from wild magic, in the end. It's the oldest, purest kind of magic. It sounds scary. I bet it will be Kit's favorite.

"There are magical animals with enough wild magic to power a city," said Faith. "I can promise, you wouldn't want to meet them on a dark night."

Kit immediately wanted to meet all of them. She opened her mouth to ask what kinds of magical animals had lots of wild magic, but Josh got in another question first.

"I've got the first six types—including wild magic. But what's the seventh kind of magic?"

Faith continued her explanation.

7. **Mind**: Magic that controls people's minds and alters what they remember. It's not QUITE as dangerous as wild magic, but still scary. Affecting other people's minds in a serious way can go VERY wrong. That's why Faith didn't want

to use a mindwipe spell on us. She also said that affecting your OWN mind is bad, too. Like, one wizard tried to make herself cleverer and she drove herself insane instead. I'm glad I'm already clever.

"Kit," said Faith, "do you have any questions about your powers?"

Josh opened his mouth.

"I said Kit," warned Faith.

Kit thought about this. "Why did I get my powers so early?"

Faith looked thoughtful. "Honestly? I'm not sure. It's possible that your powers came when they did because the world's wild magic knew that you were needed."

"Nice to feel wanted," said Kit. "Even by wild magic."

Faith smiled. "Well, no matter what awoke your powers, you'll need to learn how to use them."

"So what happens next? How do I learn to use them?"

"I need to speak to the Wizards' Council," said Faith. "If they say yes, I'll train you. They're the . . . Well, I imagine they would say they're my bosses. I'm not sure I agree. Anyway, they make sure all the wizards don't misuse magic and generally keep an eye on things."

"They sound like teachers," said Kit. She didn't like the sound of them.

Faith smiled. "A little. Though, with an average age of a hundred and two, they're a bit older than most teachers."

The children's eyes widened. "Wow. My gran is sixty, and she's the oldest person I've ever met," said Josh. "She's so old, she remembers what it was like before the internet!"

Faith let out a little coughing laugh. "The members of the Wizards' Council are definitely older than the internet. A couple of them are still adjusting to the idea of television. And the Chairwizard is even a bit iffy about radio." She stirred the jug of lemonade, making the ice clink. The whole room smelled of citrus. "Anyway, as soon as I've spoken to them, I'll start training you."

"Shouldn't she go to . . . wizard school or something?" asked Josh, sounding disappointed.

Faith poured out lemonade for everyone and shook her head.

"Kit can't go to the Wizard Academy yet—that's for eighteen-year-olds who've already finished regular school. I'll have to train you myself. In a less"—Faith waved her hand—"formal way."

"What am I training *for*, though?" asked Kit.

"Oh, you know. Running the library. Saving the world from evil. That sort of thing."

The lemonade might not have been magic, but it definitely tasted like it was. It was syrupy sweet and cold and made Kit's entire mouth zing.

"Mmmm," said Kit. "That's delic— Wait, saving the world from *what*?"

"Evil," said Faith.

"Evil what? Evil wizards?" asked Josh.

Faith nodded. "Among other things."

"Are there a lot of evil wizards?" asked Alita.

"A few, yes," said Faith. "Dogon! No!"

Dogon was sniffing at Alita's glass. He ignored Faith, but when Alita shook her head and wagged her finger, he lowered his head apologetically and was soon snuggled into a snoring ball on her lap. Faith looked impressed.

"I wouldn't worry about evil wizards for now," Faith went on, taking a sip of her own lemonade. "The first step is to help you gain control of your powers and learn some spells. And, of course, learn how the library works. Which is at least half of a wizard's job."

"Why *do* wizards work in libraries?" asked Alita.

Faith looked at her. "It's our duty to guard . . . Well, let's say to keep things running smoothly.

Also, we need the money. Wizards still have to pay bills, you know."

"Couldn't you cast a spell to make people think you've paid your bills?" suggested Josh.

Faith gave him a horrified look. "That's the kind of thing *evil* wizards do! What a thought!" She peered closer at him. "Are *you* evil, Josh? Should I be talking to your parents?"

Josh looked at his hands. "Just trying to be helpful," he mumbled. "Not evil. Please don't tell my mom."

But Faith started laughing. "It's OK. I'm just messing with you. You look about as evil as Dogon there."

Faith turned to Kit. "How do you feel about training with me for the rest of the summer? Or are you going away?"

Kit shook her head. She hadn't gone on vacation for years—there were too many people in her family to fit anywhere, except camping, and her parents *hated* camping. They had no idea where Kit got her love of the outdoors.

"Right then, shall we say ten a.m. tomorrow?" asked Faith.

"Can we come?" asked Josh.

"Of course. It's a public library!" said Faith. "And Kit will probably need a little help keeping her feet on the ground. And I mean that figuratively. I won't be teaching her levitation spells for a while."

"What does *figuratively* mean?" asked Kit.

"It's the opposite of literally," explained Josh.

"And *literally* is?" asked Kit, wanting to hit Josh for talking in circles.

"There's a dictionary on the shelf over there," said Faith. She pointed to a row of heavy books in a corner of the common room. "You can look things up whenever you like."

"I don't see why I should be punished for Josh being annoying," grumbled Kit.

"What's wizard training like?" asked Josh, ignoring her.

Faith answered all of Josh's questions patiently. Much more patiently than Kit would have.

Wizardry (or is it wizardness? Wizardosity? Anyway, being a wizard) isn't something that you get from your parents. It's random. So anyone could be born with magic powers. Most of the time, the first you know about it is when a wizard comes to find you. Young wizards usually then do an apprenticeship—which is a bit like working but also a bit like school—before their powers start working.

Adult wizards find out about most young wizards

because there's a secret, invisible question put into school exams. The school librarian—aka the school wizard!—adds an extra question that's invisible unless you have magical potential. The question is usually just something normal, but it's the fact that you can see it that matters.

So maybe there's still hope for me! I'm really looking forward to my exams when I'm a teenager now! Even more than I was before! Exams are the best!

After everyone had finished their lemonade, Faith walked them out of the stacks and back to the ordinary part of the library. Dogon stayed in the corridor of tree books, but not before giving Alita a goodbye lick on the cheek, making her giggle.

"That's gross!" said Josh. "It's also dangerous. You remember he breathes fire, right?"

"It's cute!" said Alita. "Bye, Dogon!"

They emerged into the bright lighting of the main library. Kit thought it all looked absolutely . . . normal. Shouldn't the world look different now?

All the way home, Josh and Alita talked about what they'd seen and what it meant.

"This is huge," Josh said. "This changes everything."

"We know this enormous secret," said Alita. "Something almost no one else knows. I've never had a secret this big before! The toilet thing is nothing compared to this!"

"I'm still hungry," said Kit. "Should we go to my house for a snack?"

"Aren't you too excited to eat?" asked Alita.

Kit looked at her as if she'd grown an extra head. "What does being excited have to do with being hungry? I can be both!"

"You don't seem that excited," said Josh.

Kit shrugged. She was excited. But putting it into words felt . . . too big. How did you explain something like that? Her tongue felt tangled just thinking about it, like earbuds that had been in your pocket too long and wrapped around and around themselves in a nest of chaos.

When they got home, Kit's parents were busy feeding the baby. Well, Kit's mom was feeding Baby while her dad stopped Toddler from breaking things and putting gloopy things inside other things that shouldn't have gloopy things inside them, like ears—or the DVD player.

Kit's mom glanced up from spooning goop into Baby's mouth.

"Oh, hello, Kit. You look very clean!"

"We were at the library," said Kit.

"Not the cemetery?" asked her father. "Please

don't put that up your nose. It's not meant to go up your nose. Nothing's meant to go up your nose except air. Your nose is for down and out only."

It took a moment for Kit to realize he wasn't talking to her.

"Can we have some food?" she asked.

Her mother gestured to the kitchen counter, where there were some sandwiches, then turned back to Baby.

Clearly no one had given her mom the message that Kit was Special.

Kit, Josh, and Alita took their sandwiches, along with some orange juice and fruit, and went upstairs to Kit's bedroom.

"If Dogon were here, we could make these into toasted sandwiches," said Alita.

"Hey, maybe you can learn some spells that do that? Like, fire spells?" said Josh.

Kit's eyes lit up. "Fire spells, yesssssss." She took a bite of sandwich. "I wonder why wizards run the library. Faith didn't really say. I mean, if they want to fight evil wizards, shouldn't they have a super-cool fortress with armor and shields and stuff?"

"Maybe they have invisible shields?" suggested Alita.

"Maybe that's why those doors are so hard to get into? Maybe that *is* a shield," said Josh.

"Or maybe the doors are just broken?" said Kit.

"You've got no imagination," Josh said grumpily.

"No, but I've got magic powers," pointed out Kit. "Apparently." She looked at her hands. "I don't feel magical."

"Maybe that comes later?" said Josh. "Maybe you only start feeling magical when you start learning spells?"

"We'll find out more tomorrow, won't we?" said Alita. "I can't wait!"

CHAPTER 5

TRAINING DAY

When Kit arrived at the library to start her training the next morning, she wasn't quite sure what to expect. She didn't know how wizards trained. Perhaps it was like learning martial arts—you had to practice moves. Perhaps she'd be learning some spells by heart. Maybe—*THUMP!*

"Here." Faith plonked a huge pile of books onto a desk in one corner of the library. "These books need shelving. You just need to match the number on the spine to the number on one of the shelves. There's a list of where you'll find each number, but I'm sure you'll get the hang of it quickly."

Kit looked down at the pile of books. "But . . . aren't we going to do spells? Did you talk to the Wizards' Council? Am I allowed to do magic?"

"I'll give you a hint. The answer rhymes with *mess*," said Faith.

"Yessss!" said Kit. "Awesome! What else did they say?"

"They said a lot about how the existence of such a young wizard was 'unheard of' and 'shocking.' Then one of them said, 'Gladys, give me my pills. I think I'm going to have a heart attack.' He didn't, though, luckily," said Faith. "Have a heart attack, I mean. Because Gladys *did* give him his pills. But I don't think I've seen them this excited since I took cake to the last council meeting. What was I saying?" Faith shook her head, locs whipping back and forth. "Phew. Their long-windedness is contagious."

"You were saying something about me doing spells?"

"Ah, right," said Faith. "What I was going to say was, you're allowed to do spells as long as you get the hang of the library first. It's just as important as magic."

"But—" said Kit.

Faith held up a finger. "Shhh. And later," she went on, "you can help with storytime."

"Story time? But . . . when am I going to learn to do magic?"

"When I think you're ready," said Faith. "Now, go on." She made a shooing motion toward the pile of books. Alita and Josh were already enthusiastically digging through them, checking the numbers on the spines against the list of shelves.

"But I'm a wizard. It's not fair." Kit turned back to Faith, but the librarian was gone. "This isn't magic," she finished.

"No. But it's books!" said Josh. "Look at all these books! I haven't even heard of any of these."

"Me neither," said Alita. "Look, this one's about zombies! I'm not allowed to read books about zombies. Which must mean they're good books. Adults never bother telling you not to read the boring ones."

"I've got one about knitting here," said Josh. "No

one's ever told me not to read about knitting." He pulled the book open. "Yeah . . . and I can see why."

The two of them picked up armfuls of books and scurried about the library.

Kit sighed and picked up a book. It was about the Second World War and had a boring-looking black-and-white photo on the cover. She noted the number on its spine, checked the list, then wandered over to the NONFICTION section.

When she'd put the book back in its correct place, she wandered slowly back to the table. On the way, she passed the office at the side of the library. She spotted a familiar book on the table. A book about gardens.

Well, I'm sure Faith would want me to reshelve that . . .

She picked it up.

Remembering what had happened last time, Kit took the book off to a reading corner and propped it up on a beanbag chair. She looked around to make sure no one was watching and began to read, this time from the beginning.

She was standing in a garden. This time the garden had a lush green lawn and tall trees all around it. A fountain tinkled. She could smell freshly mown grass.

Kit grinned. This was better than shelving books. And she could go back to work in a few minutes.

She strolled around the garden, bending down to peer into a pool full of large fish. At the edge of the garden, there was a thick woodland grove. She walked through the trees and found herself in an open meadow littered with wildflowers.

"I shouldn't stay too long," she said to herself. "I might just have a little nap on this soft grass. I'll just close my eyes for a moment . . ."

With a start, Kit woke up. She had no idea how long she'd been asleep. She felt dazed and fuzzy around the edges. And she wasn't in the same garden that she'd fallen asleep in.

Her heart was thumping. What if she got stuck here? What had Faith said about spending too long in one place? She couldn't think. Her mind felt like mud. *What was the spell? The spell to get back to the library?*

"House"? Is that what Faith had said? No, it wasn't quite *house* . . . but it sounded like it. And how had she moved her hands when she did the spell?

Now that she needed to, Kit didn't feel entirely confident that she remembered. But she had to try. She said the spell and waved her hands like Faith had done.

A bit like Faith had done, anyway.

"HOUZZ!" she cried.

Nothing happened.

"HAUS?"

There was a rustling sound from the trees. Something was coming.

Kit backed up a few paces across the smooth green lawn.

Something was coming through the trees. Something on stompy feet. Something large.

The rustling became a crashing. Then a huge creature lurched out from between the trees.

No, it wasn't a creature. It was a house. A house on legs. Giant chicken legs, in fact.

The house was coming straight for her.

Kit began to run, but she tripped. The house was almost on her.

"Stop right there!" came a voice. "Bad house! You're not supposed to be here!"

The house on legs stopped. Kit looked up from the ground to see Faith standing there, point-ing at the house. Her eyes glinted with fury.

The house made a whimper-ing sound, and its chicken legs sagged at the knees.

"This isn't even your section. Go back to fairy

tales immediately!" Faith crisscrossed the air with both hands. *"Reverso!"*

The house disappeared with a loud *POP!*

Faith turned to Kit with an expression that was only slightly less stern than the one she'd turned on the house. "Now. Let's get you back. And then we can have a *talk*," said Faith. *"Hus!"*

Ah, that *was what the spell was*, thought Kit.

They were back in the library, in the back office. Faith was glaring at Kit. Josh and Alita were staring at her accusingly.

"You've been gone for ages! I can't believe you sneaked into the book without us!" said Josh.

"He means he can't believe you sneaked into the book when you're supposed to be shelving," corrected Alita.

"You didn't tell me *not* to go into the book, though," said Kit.

"I didn't think I had to," said Faith. "I also didn't tell you not to juggle with piranhas. And, you'll notice, I didn't think it was necessary to warn you not to jump off a mountain without a parachute.

I had you down as someone who could figure out things like that for yourself."

"Sorry," said Kit.

Faith shrugged. "Well. You were nearly trampled by Baba Yaga's house, so hopefully I won't have to tell you not to do it again."

"Baba Who?" Kit's heart was still racing. She reminded herself that she was safe in the library now. Her head was starting to clear. She took a deep breath of dusty, reassuring air.

"Baba Yaga is a fairy-tale witch who has a house on chicken legs," said Josh. He gave a sniff. "Everyone knows that."

"Do you have to be such a know-it-all?" asked Kit.

"I'm not a know-it-all," objected Josh. "I just know it all. There's a difference."

Faith was looking at Kit curiously. "How *did* you manage to summon the house?"

Kit shrugged, feeling embarrassed. She knew she shouldn't have done it. She didn't even really know *how* she'd done it. "I . . . thought I did the spell you did to leave the book last time."

"You clearly didn't, or you wouldn't have been chased by a house on chicken legs that belongs in a fairy tale," said Faith.

Kit couldn't meet Faith's gaze. "I . . . suppose I did it wrong?"

"And then some," said Faith. She snorted. "Doing spells inside a portal book, when you don't know what you're doing, is *very* dangerous. I suppose I have to punish you now, so you know not to do something so dangerous again. I can't say I've ever had to deal with a misbehaving child wizard before, so I don't know how hard on you to be." She tilted her head and looked Kit up and down.

"You could punish me by making me do really hard spells! Some fireballs, maybe? I'd really hate that!" suggested Kit.

Faith let out a loud laugh. "I'm a wise and cunning wizard. What part of that makes you think I'll punish you by making you do *exactly what you want*?"

Kit blushed. "Uh . . . "

"Listen," said Faith. "Not all wizards have long

white beards and no clue about the real world, you know."

Unfortunately for Faith, just at that moment, an old man with a white beard walked past muttering to himself. "Pixies . . . must remember to feed the pixies . . ."

The children looked at Faith. Faith rolled her eyes.

"OK, but we're not all like him," said Faith. "That's Greg, the assistant librarian. He's mostly retired, but he still comes in to help out from time to time." She nodded over toward the children's section of the library. "Come on. I'll think of a suitable punishment later. It's story time." She pointed to Kit. "You can do the reading."

"Oh," said Kit, with terror in her heart. "I—"

"I think you've found the right punishment," said Alita. "Kit hates reading out loud."

"Especially in front of people," added Josh. "Wow. Those kids look very impatient." He pointed. A knot of small children were sitting on the floor in a corner of the children's section, looking restless and eager.

Reading out loud was truly Kit's nightmare. Worse than being attacked by spiders (that was just tickly), and worse than finding out your lunch had mold on it (you can always eat around mold). Worse than swimming with sharks when you have a cut on your foot and a sign around your neck saying TASTES JUST LIKE SEAL!

"You mean I have to read . . . to all those children?" asked Kit. Her eyes were wide. "So many of them? All . . . looking at me?"

Faith put a hand on her shoulder. "You'll be fine. Alita, would you like to pick a story for Kit to read?"

Alita hurried off excitedly and returned with a book about a princess riding a unicorn into battle against goblins. She handed it to Kit.

Kit opened it, glancing fearfully at the pages. At least there were plenty of pictures and not too many long words.

"Are unicorns real?" she heard Alita ask.

Faith nodded. "Yes. But whatever you do, don't try to ride one. That never ends well. Grumpy creatures. Very pointy horns."

Faith strode to Kit's side and beamed at the audience of waiting children, pushing her locs behind her shoulders with a flourish.

"Hello, children! This is Kit. She's going to read the story today. And she's going to do *all* the voices."

The children beamed back at her.

Kit's stomach sank. Reading out loud was hard enough without having to figure out what a unicorn's voice was supposed to sound like.

"Remember, children, no clapping at the end. This is a library." Faith put her finger to her lips. All the children copied her.

Kit hoped they wouldn't riot when they realized how terrible she was at reading.

CHAPTER 6

WHO NEEDS LIBRARIES?

The next fifteen minutes were horrible. Torture. Humiliation. A nightmare.

Kit stumbled over words. The children looked bored. One of them kept calling out to complain that she was doing the voices wrong. At one point, Josh started to walk up to the front to take over, until Alita sat on him. "You've got to let her try!" Kit heard Alita whisper, which only made her stumble more.

But eventually the torture was over. The children didn't clap. And not because they were being good, quiet, obedient library-goers.

"That was terrible," groaned Kit. She handed the book back to Faith.

Faith refused it. "You know how to shelve it, Kit. And that wasn't terrible. You just need practice. No one starts off good at everything. You get good by doing."

"I've never gotten good at anything," said Kit.

"Have you tried at anything?" asked Faith.

Kit didn't have a reply to that, so she changed the subject.

"What should I do now?" she asked. She was getting hungry and tired. This was supposed to be summer vacation, and she was supposed to be a wizard. But she'd spent the whole day shelving books and reading to children. Well, OK, she'd spent at least an hour doing those things. But she already felt like she'd run a marathon wearing metal boots while doing math problems in her head.

Faith took one look at her face and said, "I think it's time for a break. Lemonade? Perhaps some ginger cake?"

"Both, please!" said Josh.

"Can we go see Dogon?" asked Alita.

"Of course. I think he's been pining for you," said Faith. "He's started shedding scales from his chest—though that might be because he's due for a molting."

Alita's eyes widened. "Wow! Like a snake? Let's go and see him now before we miss it!"

Faith smiled. "Of course. Come on, children."

"HELLO?" yelled a man's voice. "SERVICE?"

Kit jumped. In the library, everything was hushed and calm. But this man sounded as if he were shouting to be heard over the noise of a herd of elephants having a dance party on a highway.

Kit turned to see a middle-aged man standing near the library desk, wearing a close-fitting suit and a bright-red tie with a diamond-studded tie-pin. His black shoes were so highly polished, the sun glinted off them.

The man had a bushy mustache and a pile of dry brown hair on his head that looked like a bird's nest made out of steel wool. It looked like hair a robot might weave out of scratchy metal if it had never seen real human hair but had once read a book about it, in the dark.

As Kit and the others approached the desk, the man scowled at them.

"Took you long enough!" he spat. His puffy face was very, very pink, as though some- one had mixed stomach medicine with cotton candy. His mustache looked like a caterpillar crossed with a bath mat. Or possibly a caterpillar *fighting* a bath mat. It twitched as he spoke.

"How can I help you?" asked Faith in a low, quiet voice.

"I'm Hadrian Salt!" he

boomed. "I'm the CEO and president of Hadrian Salt Enterprises. You might have seen my building? It's the largest and the most incredible building in town. Made entirely out of glass and gold."

"That's nice," said Faith. "Can I help you find a book?"

Salt gave a snorting laugh, like a pig with a blocked nose. "A BOOK? Me? Oh, no. Definitely not. I'm here for your signature."

"But she's not famous," said Josh.

Salt threw back his head and laughed again. "Not that kind of signature, you silly child," he said.

"Don't call Josh a silly child," said Kit. "He's read every book in the school library!"

"I have!" said Josh.

"Only weaklings read books themselves." Salt sniffed. "I pay people to read *for* me." He pulled out a piece of paper and a pen and held them out to Faith. "I need your signature on this contract to acknowledge that I will be taking possession of this building. I'm buying the library. It's all agreed with the city council, but apparently I need your signature as a formality." He shook the paper at her. "Sign here!" He grunted and shoved the pen at Faith again. "Sign! I haven't got all day!"

Faith didn't take the pen. "What are you talking about? The library's not for sale. I'm not signing anything. I think you should leave. You're talking too loudly." She gestured at the QUIET sign. "This is a library."

"Not for long," brayed Salt. He gestured around at the books. "When Hadrian Salt Enterprises takes over, we'll soon get rid of all this and replace it with something wonderful. A shopping center, perhaps. Who needs libraries these days? We have the internet!"

"*We* need libraries," said Alita.

"And I hate shopping," said Kit.

"And anyway," said Faith, "as I said, the library is not for sale. Please put away your pen."

"OH, REALLY?" said Salt. "That's how you want

to play it, do you? Well, I'm sure I can find a way around getting your signature. Details, details . . ."

He glowered, his pink face turning gradually redder with fury. His mustache seemed to bristle.

He wasn't the only one getting angry. Kit wasn't sure, but she thought Faith was starting to glow a little. Purple sparks crackled around her eyes.

Salt didn't seem to notice, or at least he didn't care. He sniffed. "You're just delaying what will happen anyway, you know."

The sparks around Faith's eyes flashed more brightly.

Salt started to back away.

"Well. I'm an important businessman. I have important businessman things to do. I can't waste my day chatting with children and librarians. But you haven't heard the last of me. This quiet library . . . soon it will ROAR with the sound of commerce."

He backed away farther. And faster. And soon he was scuttling out the library doors.

"What a horrible man," said Faith. The crackling

light around her eyes began to fade, but she still looked furious.

"Can he do that?" asked Alita. "Buy the library?"

Faith didn't reply. She was looking gloomy. Her eyes had stopped sparking completely now.

"Children, I think you'll have to come back tomorrow. I have . . . a lot to think about."

"What should we do?" asked Kit.

But Faith had turned on her heel and stalked off toward the back of the library, heading for the stacks.

"Well, she's grumpy today," said Josh. "She never even gave us lemonade. Or cake!"

"She's worried about the library," said Alita. "Honestly, for a genius you can be quite dense, Josh."

Kit had a thought. "If that man buys the library and gets rid of all the books, does that mean I won't have to do any more shelving?"

Alita and Josh glared at her.

"I'm not saying I think it would be *good* if he bought the library and knocked it down, just . . . trying to look for an upside?"

Alita and Josh turned around and started to walk away.

"Wait for me!" said Kit. "I was just kidding. I love the books, really! Even the ones with unicorns and long words! I promise I don't want all the books to be taken away. Mostly . . . "

CHAPTER 7

SAVE THE LIBRARY!

The next morning, Faith looked awful. Her cheeks were hollow, and her eyes were narrowed. Her skin had a grayish tinge, and there were dark circles beneath her eyes. She looked like someone who'd been up all night.

Kit wanted to ask if she was OK, but she didn't want to sound rude. So as they walked through the stacks, past the book trees, she asked, "What should we do?"

"We could do a protest," suggested Alita. "They did that for the other local library."

"But didn't that close?" said Kit.

"We could do it better," said Josh.

"Isn't there something more we could do?" asked Kit. She was hoping maybe Faith could turn Salt into a frog.

"What about the Wizards' Council?" asked Josh. "Are they going to help?"

Faith made an apologetic face. "No, they're not. It's not technically a magical threat, they said, so it's not their business. They'll just keep an eye on things to make sure they don't get out of hand."

"But . . . but . . . don't they care about all their magical books? And"—Kit gestured around at the book trees—"all this?"

"They do. It's just . . . complicated."

That's what grown-ups always say when they don't want to do something, Kit thought.

"The thing is," Faith went on, "from their point of view, it's not something they should meddle in. For now, it's just an ordinary man building a shopping center. A very annoying man. But still, he's not an evil wizard, so it's against the rules for them to fight him."

"Oh," said Kit, swallowing.

"They said if they got involved with every non-magical threat, they'd end up secretly running the whole world. And when wizards try to run the world, it never ends well," said Faith.

"Oooh, when did they try to run the world?" asked Josh, getting out his notebook.

Faith gave him a look. "Wizard history lesson later, Josh. I'm a little tired."

Once they were settled in armchairs with glasses of ice-cold lemonade, Faith seemed to relax.

"Can't we tell Salt the truth?" suggested Kit. "That we're wizards, and this is where we keep the magic books, and that we need the library?"

Kit wanted to add, *Because I haven't even trained properly yet, so it can't all be over before it's begun,* but that sounded too selfish.

Faith was already shaking her head. "Magic is secret. I swore an oath."

"But there must be something we can do," said Kit.

Faith pinched the bridge of her nose. "I think it's

best if I deal with this. It's all very complicated and delicate."

And I'm a big clumsy elephant who'll only ruin it all, thought Kit gloomily.

"Can we organize a protest at least?" she asked.

"With banners," added Josh. "I can write really straight letters!"

"I can get all my family to help," said Alita. "My mom knows *everyone* around here. She could help spread the word."

Faith thought about this. "Of course, that's fine. Just don't try to talk to Salt. Leave that to me." She gave a very strained smile. "Why don't I teach you your first spell, Kit? Starting tomorrow. It will help you make your banners."

CHAPTER 8

THE SPARKLY SPELL

When Kit got to the library the next morning, Josh and Alita had been there for a while already—they'd finished their *Wizard of Earthsea* books and were disappointed to discover that the new Danny Fandango copies hadn't been returned yet.

"Why do people read so slowly?" complained Josh.

"I think they're part snail," said Alita. Then she thought about it for a moment. "Actually, being part snail might be cool. You could go camping in your own shell."

When Faith found them, she whisked them all down to the stacks. Green sunshine was streaming down between the book trees. Or perhaps it wasn't sun. They were underground, after all. But it was light, and it felt warm on Kit's face as they walked.

"Right! In here, all of you." Faith gestured toward a tall, wide tree ahead. High, high in the branches was a tiny tree house made from living branches. It looked more doll's house than human house, about a foot high and a foot wide, with branches weaving in and out of one another to form walls. The roof was covered in leaves made from book pages.

"It's a bit small," said Kit doubtfully.

"It's a bit high," said Josh fearfully.

"Awww, it's adorable!" said Alita.

"It's not as small as it looks," said Faith. "And don't worry, you don't have to climb. There's an elevator."

"Where?" asked Kit.

Faith beckoned them to follow her to the tree. There were words etched into its trunk. Faith rested a hand on the bark. She muttered two words, and a light glowed around her hand. Then a door shot open in the trunk of the tree. Inside was a wood-paneled room. "Come in."

The children crowded in, and Faith pressed a button on the wall. The elevator shot upward with a whistling whoosh and the sound of tinkling bells. Then, with a jerk, it stopped and started to slide sideways.

The elevator came to another sudden stop, which made Josh fall on top of Alita, who fell on top of Kit, who decided her friends were heavier than they looked. Faith pressed another button, and a door opened into a large room about the size of Kit's living room and bedroom put together. The walls were made of woven branches, and the floor was covered in soft, spongy moss.

The children all rushed to the windows and looked down. Beneath them the forest spread as far as the eye could see.

"How can we *fit* in here?" asked Kit, looking around at the large room, which had definitely not looked large enough from the outside to fit one human, never mind four with room for more.

"Like the forest, it's made from books come back to life," said Faith. "So, like any book, it contains whole worlds, not just the narrow distance between the covers."

"You could've just said 'it's bigger on the inside,'" said Kit.

"That's someone else's line," said Faith. "Now, let's make some banners . . . and do some magic."

The branch-walls were lined with drawers, which turned out to contain art supplies—paints, paper, large rolls of fabric, cardboard, glitter, pens, scissors, and everything else you could imagine. There was a sink for washing brushes, smocks to cover clothes, and a large wooden table and chairs that grew out of the floor.

Faith pulled open drawer after drawer, bringing out paper, fabric, cardboard, pens, and paint.

Kit and the others got down to making banners. Well, Josh and Alita made banners. Kit mostly made a mess.

After they'd made a few, Kit had to admit that Josh's and Alita's were much better than hers. They were neater, for a start. And she realized after the third SAVE THE LIBRARY sign that she'd been spelling it LYBRARY. But she thought that everyone would know what she was talking about.

"Now, Kit, let me show you something." Faith picked up one of the already-dry banners and breathed on it. Then she muttered, *"Beffrey!"*

The banner began to sparkle.

"Wow!" said Kit.

"Shiny!" said Alita.

"What type of magic is that?" asked Josh. He pulled out his notebook.

"Josh, stop badgering Faith. I want to do some actual magic!" said Kit.

"I'll give you some books on magical theory, Josh," said Faith. "Now, let's see what Kit can do." Faith handed Kit another banner. "Your very first spell. Are you ready?"

Kit snatched the banner and blurted out, *"Beffrey!"*

Nothing happened.

"You have to breathe on the poster first," said Faith. "That tells the magic which thing you want to do the spell on."

Kit breathed on the banner, on the dried paint and the wonky letters, on the thin cloth . . . and then she said the word. More confidently this time. A little too confidently.

"BEFFREY!"

The banner burst into a shower of burning sparks and vanished.

"AAARGH!" yelled Kit.

The others jumped back.

Faith laughed. "It's fine. You're fine. That kind of thing often happens when you're learning. Try again. More quietly—and perhaps a little closer to the sink, just in case."

It took a few tries before Kit managed to make the spell work. The next time she tried, nothing happened. The time after that, as she spoke a *little* louder, she saw a few faint glints across the cloth, as if someone had spilled glitter a few weeks ago and then dropped the banner on the floor.

In the end, the fifth time was the charm.

She breathed on the cloth, said the word, and felt a rush of power wash over her, like a warm wave across her heart.

The cloth in her hands began to sparkle.

Josh and Alita clapped.

"Well done," said Faith. She crossed to a cupboard and rummaged for a moment, then came out with a piece of white cloth. She held it out to Kit. It shimmered as it moved, like silk in moonlight.

"Put it on," said Faith.

Kit put the cloth around her shoulders like a superhero and did it up with the little silver clasp that sat at the neck of the cloak. It came down almost to the ground.

"A wizard's cloak!" cried Alita and Josh.

Kit swooshed the cloak back and forth. It made a very satisfying sound, like the swooping wings of a great bird.

"Technically, trainee wizards are supposed to wear short cloaks," said Faith. "But that cloak was designed for an eighteen-year-old at the Wizard Academy. Perhaps you could have it taken up so it doesn't get in the way?"

"I like it!" said Kit. Then she looked at Faith. "Why aren't you wearing a cloak?"

"I only wear mine for special occasions and ceremonies," said Faith. "But it's useful for you to wear yours as you train, because it tracks your progress. Look." She pointed to the hem of the white cloak. A faint yellow line had appeared near the bottom.

"What's that?" asked Kit.

"That's a record of your first spell. As you learn more, your cloak will change color. You gain a yellow stripe for each new basic spell until your cloak is wholly yellow. Then you start getting brown stripes on the yellow until your cloak is brown. Then you get green stripes and . . . well, and so on."

"Wow," said Kit. "I can't wait to get more stripes."

"Well, if you practice *beffrey* a few more times, your first yellow stripe will get darker, so you can do that for a start!"

"Yesssss," said Kit.

"What color is *your* cloak?" Josh asked Faith.

"Wouldn't you like to know," said Faith. "Now, Kit, you practice your spell. You two, make banners. You have a protest to organize."

She was smiling, but there was something a little strained about her face, thought Kit. Did Faith really think this protest was going to stop Salt?

CHAPTER 9

THE YELLOWING CLOAK

It took a few days to spread the word about the protest. Kit told her family and asked them to tell everyone they knew. Alita told her mom, and Alita wasn't kidding about her knowing everyone. Her mom was like a one-woman internet, making information whizz around town at the speed of light. Or however fast things moved on the internet. Kit wasn't sure.

When she wasn't helping her friends spread the word, Kit learned more spells. Faith taught her one or two a day—"You can't take in too much at once. You have to learn each one confidently before you move on to the next, or it'll fuddle your brains."

Kit had to admit, her brain was feeling pretty full. It wasn't just about remembering the words of each spell—although they were often very short, just one or two words, there were also all the gestures to remember.

She wore her cloak as she trained. It was *very* satisfying to see the yellow lines appear, and it wasn't long before the bottom two inches or so of her cloak were a solid yellow.

One day she learned a spell that helped her hear quiet conversations. ("Very important in a library," said Faith.) This involved making a complicated hand gesture. First Kit touched her lips, then the air in front of her, and then she had to hold her fingers in a particular way, raising two, then balling up the others, with her thumb on top. It was fiddly to get right. Then, while touching her lips, she had to say, *"Broadcast the quiet, ymhelaethu!"*—which was a real mouthful.

The first time she tried it, nothing happened. The second time, she just heard her own heartbeat thumping in her ears freakishly loud. But it worked the third time—she was able to hear someone whispering on the other side of the library.

She also learned spells for:

- Landing softly without hurting herself if she fell over. (Useful for tree climbing.)
- Remembering someone's birthday. (With four siblings, two parents, four grand-parents, and about nine million cousins, Kit thought that one was going to be a lifesaver.)
- Elemental spells, including making a spark of fire shoot from her fingers. (Kit was under strict instructions to only do that one when Faith was around, and not

near any books, or paper, or any of Faith's possessions.)

- Turning porridge into chocolate. (Faith insisted that she should only do that on special occasions, as spells that unrot teeth were very hard.)
- Making small objects invisible. (Making *yourself* invisible was apparently a very high-level spell.) Kit managed to make a stapler, a shoe, and a mug invisible. Unfortunately it was Faith's favorite mug, and they had to wait two days for it to wear off before she could drink out of it again.

In the afternoons, after spell practice, Faith always hurried off—sometimes down into the stacks, and sometimes she just seemed to vanish.

"Perhaps she's having meetings with the city council to stop them from selling the library?" suggested Alita.

"Maybe she's going to persuade the Wizards' Council to help?" suggested Josh.

Kit found it annoying that Faith never said where she was going, looking so worried and in a hurry. But they had other things to keep them busy.

Kit, Alita, and Josh went door-to-door and handed out leaflets that Kit had printed at home. Some people slammed the door. Others nodded and smiled politely while clearly balling up the leaflet to throw in the recycling bin. But a lot of people who lived nearby seemed worried about the library.

"It's somewhere warm to go," said one old man. "And there are people."

"It's somewhere to get all the books I can't afford to buy," said one girl.

"It's somewhere where I'm not the only nerd," said a little boy.

And a lot of people promised to show up to the protest.

"We should invite Salt, too," said Faith. "And people from the city council. They might not come, but it can't hurt."

So they sent out invitations and spread the word, and soon the day of the protest arrived.

CHAPTER 10

THE LIBRARY PROTEST

Lots of people turned up on Saturday. Alita's family was all there, along with friends, neighbors, and even a few people Alita's mom had met on the way.

Kit, Josh, and Alita waved their sparkling banners. People in the crowd came up with funny chants about Salt and serious chants about why libraries mattered. It was all going very well until Salt himself showed up.

A woman was giving a speech about how she came to the library with her children every week, and that they were able to read all the books they'd never be able to read otherwise, when Salt strode onto the stage and snatched the microphone from her.

"Hello, whiners!" he bellowed. "I can't believe what a sad bunch of people you are, wasting your Saturday doing THIS." He gestured at the protest. "I want to do you the favor of telling you it's all pointless. The deal is done. I take possession in two days. I'll soon be looking down on this library from my penthouse office in my incredibly shiny tower, knowing that it's my property. It's my fiftieth birthday tomorrow. It will be SUCH an excellent birthday present. So you're all wasting your time. Why don't you go shopping and spend money? That's what real, ordinary people like to do on the weekend. Unlike you book-thumping snobs."

"I don't have any money!" someone from the crowd shouted.

"We like the library!" called someone else.

Salt just snorted, flaring his pink nostrils. "Go on. Clear out, all of you. This library belongs to ME!"

The crowd booed.

But then a gang of security guards in matching blue uniforms came out of Salt's building down the street and marched toward the crowd menacingly.

"My security team will move you along if you don't go away," yelled Salt.

"You can't do this!" someone shouted.

"I can. I already have," spat back Salt. "It's my private property! Or it will be very soon, so you can clear out!"

The security guards started shoving the nearest people in the crowd.

One by one, the crowd thinned out, until the only people left were Faith, Kit, Alita, and Josh— along with Greg, the elderly assistant librarian.

Salt looked down at them. "Well, isn't THIS pathetic. You don't know when to give up, do you? Guards! Escort these people away."

The security guards marched closer. But Faith shook her head. "We're leaving," she said. "Come on, children. And Greg."

"This isn't over," mumbled Greg.

Faith led them into the library. Kit glanced back

at Salt, who was glaring at them. She couldn't resist sticking out her tongue at him. It didn't help. But it made her feel better.

And she did have one thought. Salt had said his office was the penthouse. Kit knew that meant the floor at the very top of the building. She wasn't sure what she could do with that information yet. But it was something.

CHAPTER 11

BENEATH THE BOOK FOREST

Inside the library, Faith took them down into the stacks and into the break room.

"What are we going to do about Salt?" asked Kit. "What can *I* do?"

Faith smiled at Kit. "For the moment? You're going to keep training."

"But Salt—" objected Kit.

"I'm working on it," said Faith. "But you can't neglect your training."

"Come on, Kit, we can help you practice your spells," said Alita.

"I know them all by heart now," said Josh. "So I can test you."

"And there's story time to do, too," said Faith. "You can't forget that."

"Can we do story time this time?" asked Josh. "Pleeeeeease?"

Faith thought about this. "Well, traditionally only wizards do, but . . ." She waved her hands. "Go for it! I have some work to do. Kit, spell practice. Josh, Alita, story time. No stories with mice in them, please."

Faith shooed them out of her office and walked off toward the stacks.

Alita went to pick out a book for story time. "I wonder why no mice?" she mused.

"Maybe some kids are scared of mice? Little kids are weird," said Josh. "My littlest sister is terrified of yogurt. *Yogurt!*"

"How about this one? Lions, but no mice."

"Hmmm. Can you do a good lion voice, though? I think I should do those parts."

"I can!"

"Bet you can't!"

"I can! *RRRROAR* . . ."

"Shh, not so loud," said Josh, pointing at the QUIET IN THE LIBRARY sign.

Kit left them bickering and went to practice her spells in a quiet corner. She went over the invisibility spell until she could do it without having to concentrate so hard that her tongue popped out of her mouth. She made a whole book invisible—a big, hardback one! She couldn't manage anything bigger than that, though.

Next, she tried a silence spell—she'd used it before to make someone's voice quiet in the library, but now she practiced by dropping a pencil sharpener without it making a sound when it landed.

When she tried the chocolate-out-of-porridge spell, she got stuck. She'd managed to find some porridge in the staff kitchen, but she couldn't seem to pronounce one of the words correctly, however many times she tried. She ended up with smears of chocolate all over her hands, but her porridge remained gray and porridgey. So she went down into the stacks to find Faith, to figure out what was going wrong.

At first, Kit couldn't find the librarian anywhere. She wasn't in the break room or in the tree house. Kit wandered around between the trees for what felt like forever, when at last she spotted her.

Faith was standing in front of one of the book trees. It was a huge tree, so wide that it would take at least three fully grown adults with their arms outstretched to wrap themselves all the way around it. Kit was about to go over to her when she realized that Faith was casting a spell.

I shouldn't interrupt her halfway through a spell, in case it goes wrong, thought Kit. More quietly, in case Faith could read her mind, she thought, *And if I don't interrupt her, I'll find out what she's up to.*

So she edged closer, trying not to draw Faith's attention. *If she spots me, she'll ask why I'm spying on her, and then she'll give me a LOOK,* thought Kit.

Faith was muttering the spell to herself, and

then she started to walk with slow, purposeful steps, each foot placed ever so carefully. She walked three times clockwise around the tree, then turned back, waving her hands once again. As she walked around the tree one last time, a door opened in the bark of the trunk. Inside, Kit could see the top of a staircase.

Faith started down the stairs. Before she could think about it, Kit followed her through the magical door. She tiptoed as quietly as she could down the white spiral staircase, going farther and farther down. At this point, she knew she was doing something wrong, but it was too late not to do it, so she might as well finish doing it. Half a wrong thing was just as bad as a whole wrong thing, Kit had found, and a lot less fun.

After descending for about ten minutes, Kit's legs were starting to ache with the effort. She felt a little dizzy. It was so bright on the staircase, and the muffled sounds made her feel very far away from herself.

But finally she reached the bottom. There was a golden door in front of her, engraved with swirling carvings that looked like snakes. There was no door handle and no keyhole. And there was no sign of Faith.

Without thinking, Kit put her hand against the door. It just felt like the right thing to do.

The door swung open, revealing a vast, high-ceilinged chamber.

In the center of the chamber lay huge piles of golden coins, jewels, shining cups—a hoard of treasure. Normally, that would have blown Kit's mind. She would have shrieked with excitement and dived into the shining piles of coins and gems. But there was something even more incredible on top of the treasure.

CHAPTER 12

THE DRAGON IN THE LIBRARY

The creature was colossal and covered with glistening green scales. Its huge horned head rested on the pile of treasure, and it appeared to be asleep.

That, thought Kit, *is a dragon.*

And it was.

She stood there for a moment gazing at the gigantic beast. It had a long face, with a nose that came to a sharp, beak-like point. Wings spread on either side of its body, sprouting from muscular green shoulders. For a moment, Kit imagined what it would look like flying over the city, flapping those wings. The thought made her stomach drop with excitement and fear.

The dragon's scaly sides were rising and falling very, very slowly. Each time it breathed out, a puff of smoke emerged from its nostrils.

Kit felt drawn toward the dragon. She could sense a hum of magic coming from it. It felt like a part of her. Before she knew it, she was kneeling down. She carefully placed her right hand on its side. Its scales were cold and a little scratchy. Her fingers began to tingle, growing warmer. She felt a rush of heat wash over her.

Then everything went dark.

Just for a moment.

Kit blinked when the light returned. She was still in the dragon's cave, but something was different.

The dragon was awake and looking at her. Its eyes were a shining green. Its sharp teeth showed between its scaly lips as it opened its mouth and roared.

"Oh!" Kit stepped backward. "Please don't eat me. I'm sorry I woke you."

"You didn't," came a voice from beside her. "The dragon's still asleep. We're in the dragon's dream. No one's getting eaten. Probably."

Kit turned to see Faith standing by her side. She

didn't look happy. But she didn't look like someone who was about to turn anyone into a toad, either. So that was a plus.

"So you followed me," said Faith.

"Slightly. A bit. Maybe. I saw you walking, and then I started walking. In the same direction. Behind you."

Faith raised an eyebrow. "Well. You're here now. We can talk about the dangers of following wizards into the unknown later."

"But . . . where *is* here?"

"Think of it as the dragon's imagination. This is where the dragon lives its life as its body sleeps. Here, anything can happen."

"Can it hurt me?"

Faith shook her head. "You've left your body in the real world. So have I. We're guests in the dragon's dream, but we're not physically here."

Kit looked around. "This is a pretty boring dream. It's just dreaming about its bedroom."

"This is only a part of my dream, wizard. My dream is vast. You're only on the doorstep." The voice was as smooth as honey and as warm as cocoa. But beneath the warmth and the smoothness was danger and fire. Kit shuddered and stepped back.

"Oh. It can talk!" she gasped.

"Not it. She."

Kit looked from the dragon to Faith to the dragon again. "How is this possible?"

"You've walked into a book, haven't you?" said the dragon. "Why not a dream? A dream and a book are very similar things, when you think about them. They both make pictures in your mind."

Kit thought the dragon was pretty weird. Then again, she didn't know what was normal for a dragon. This was the first one she'd met. Or the first-and-a-half, if you counted Dogon.

"How long have you been down here?" she asked.

"I've been here since the beginning, I think. Time passes, but I don't know how long it's been." The dragon turned its long, pointed face to Faith. "Remind me. When was that event . . . with the fire? And the burning?"

"The Great Fire of London?" offered Faith. "That was about three hundred and fifty years ago."

"That's the last time I woke up, then." The dragon blinked. "Bad things happen when I wake. The wizards keep me asleep; they tell me stories to populate the world of my dreams. They keep things quiet."

Faith approached the dragon, slowly but confidently, and rested her hand on the creature's head. "We do our best to keep the library quiet. Luckily a little noise won't wake her. But it can get a bit hairy when a very lively school trip comes to the library. And author visits. It's a good thing Draca loves stories. Even the loudest of stories don't wake her."

"It's true." The dragon showed all her teeth. Kit thought it might be a smile. "Stories make my dreams bigger. I have more space to roam."

"So that's why you had me do story time?" asked Kit.

Faith nodded. "It's an important part of your duties as a wizard. The dragon is where our power comes from, so even if it weren't dangerous for the dragon to wake, we owe her."

Kit absorbed the information that her powers came from a dragon. But then she had a thought. "So is it OK that Alita and Josh are doing story time? They're not wizards."

"It doesn't technically have to be a wizard who reads the stories. Stories are their own magic. We just need to make sure that *someone* does. So it's traditionally a wizard's duty, along with keeping the shelves tidy and all the books in their proper places."

"I don't like it when the books are out of order," said the dragon. "When someone shelves a history book with science fiction, or a gritty detective novel with the children's picture books . . ." The dragon gave a shudder. "It makes me itch. It makes me feel wakeful."

"So *that's* why we have to do shelving?" asked Kit. She suddenly felt a bit better about doing the boring stuff. Slightly.

"Shelving isn't boring," said the dragon. "It brings order to the world."

Kit felt a shudder. "You read my mind?"

"Well, you could say that. But you're in *my* dream," said the dragon. "So you *could* say I'm reading my own mind."

Kit tried to make sense of that, but it felt as though her brain was melting. She focused on things that did make sense instead. "So . . . if the dragon . . . if she . . . if you . . . wake up, why does bad stuff happen? Is it because you're grumpy when you wake up? Did you set fire to London last time you woke up? Like when I wake my big brother up before midday and he throws things?"

But the dragon gave a little whimper in the back of her great throat. "That's not fair," she said. "It wasn't my fault."

"She doesn't do it on purpose, do you, Draca?" said Faith. She turned to Kit. "When a dragon wakes, she releases a burst of magic. This magic is dangerous—it's too much power to be floating around in the world. It can change reality. It can cause plagues, earthquakes . . . and worse. But it's not the dragon's fault. It's the fault of whoever *woke* the dragon. Well, if they woke it on purpose, anyway."

"Why would anyone do that?" asked Kit. "Why would anyone cause plagues and earthquakes and stuff on purpose?"

Faith shook her head. "In my wizard training, no one's ever been able to explain that to me." She pointed to the dragon. "But I know that our duty is to protect the dragon. Keep her asleep. Keep her safe. Read her stories."

"Salt!" said Kit, suddenly afraid. "If he comes and digs up the library and builds a shopping center, he's going to wake the dragon, isn't he? The diggers would wake her!"

"Diggers!" said the dragon. "I like stories about diggers!"

"But you wouldn't like the real thing. Noisy," said Faith. "However, now that you know about the dragon, I can set your mind at ease about that, Kit. The Wizards' Council has put a temporary muffling spell around Draca. The diggers won't wake her."

"But if the library closes, we still won't be able

to come down here," said Kit. "We still have to stop him!"

"We will, I promise," said Faith. "But now we need to go. The magic required to stay here is tiring. If we stay too long, I won't be able to get us out again."

"Come back any time," said the dragon. "I like to meet people. People bring me stories."

"I will. And I promise to keep you sleeping," said Kit.

"They always say that," said the dragon sadly. "But I end up waking up in the end. I heard about another dragon, long ago, who wasn't just woken. He was killed. Then all the big lizards died." The dragon, to Kit's surprise, began to cry.

"The dinosaurs!" gasped Kit. "Killing a dragon wiped out the dinosaurs!"

"Say goodbye," said Faith. She gave a huge yawn. "Getting . . . sleepy."

Kit said goodbye to the dragon. The dragon bade her farewell.

They climbed the endless stairs, up and away from the dragon's lair. They walked slowly through the woods beneath the library, then up the slope to the revolving bookcase, until they were back in the real world.

Or as real as a world can be that has a sleeping dragon in it.

CHAPTER 13

Too Dangerous

Kit's punishment for following Faith was scraping chewing gum off the undersides of all the library tables.

"You didn't think you were getting off with a stern look, did you?" said Faith, giving her another stern look for free.

As soon as she'd finished scraping the gum, Kit went to find Josh and Alita to show them exactly why it was so important that they save the library. She had Faith's permission this time. The librarian led them all through the stacks and down to see the dragon.

Josh and Alita were amazed when they saw the creature sleeping beneath the library. They were astounded when Faith took them into her dream. They almost screamed when the dragon spoke to them.

Alita was very upset when she heard about the dragon who had been killed—the one who led to the death of the dinosaurs. She swore that she would protect this dragon from harm.

"I swear to protect you, Draca, like Lara Fandango protected the Sphinx in book four!" said Alita.

"I swear to protect you like Danny Fandango protected the good manticore in book three!" added Josh.

The dragon's huge eyes were glistening.

"You like those books?" asked Draca.

"YES!" Josh and Alita replied.

"I love it when Faith reads me Danny Fandango!" said the dragon, letting out a hiss of hot, happy breath. "Huge fan. Who's your favorite character?"

After that, it was almost impossible to get Josh

and Alita to leave. Faith had to bribe them by saying that some copies of the new book had just been returned and were upstairs.

When they returned to the book forest, Alita took Dogon up into her arms and gave him a hug.

"What if next time a dragon is killed, it wipes out all the puppies in the world?" she said. "Or all the ferrets? Or the blue whales? Or little Dogon here?"

"Or all the humans?" suggested Josh.

Alita thought about that. "Yes, that would be bad, too."

"Come on. Let's have something to drink," said Faith. "How about some ginger tea? It can get cold down in the book forest. There's a damp chill to everything."

"Then can we have our copies of the new Danny Fandango?" asked Josh, who seemed more worried about missing out on a new book than about the end of the world.

Faith nodded.

Josh and Alita made a lot of high-pitched noises and jumped up and down. Kit sighed. Sometimes her friends were basically aliens. Aliens with giant brains.

Faith started making them ginger tea in the staff room, chopping up ginger, scraping it into a pan, pouring in water, then setting it to boil while she found some cups in the cupboard and the children made themselves comfortable. Dogon was curled up on Alita's lap. The creature was snoring happily, filling the room with little puffs of smoke each time he breathed.

Kit wondered what Dogon dreamed of.

Alita stroked Dogon's fur. "How can you have a dog that's half dragon? Can dogs and dragons have babies? Is Dogon Draca's baby?"

"No, they're not related," said Faith. "Dogon is still technically a dog. I mean, he was born a dog. But being so near the dragon and its magic—it's changed him. He's absorbed some of the dragon's wild magic. Just like wizards who work here do."

"Ooh!" said Kit. "I'm absorbing wild magic?" She shuddered. "That's weird!"

Faith spooned a little sugar into the pan as it

bubbled away. When it was ready, she poured them all steaming cups of ginger tea. "One moment," she said, then passed her hands over the cups, murmuring, *"Bill . . . "* She looked up at Kit and explained, "That's a cooling spell, so you don't burn your mouth."

Kit mimed the hand gesture and was about to say the word when Faith shook her head.

"I wouldn't. If you get it wrong, you could create a new ice age. It's surprisingly powerful."

"What happens now?" asked Kit. "You said the Wizards' Council put a muffling spell around Draca. Does that mean everything's OK? It doesn't matter if Salt takes the library? Can we just, like, sneak through some tunnels or something to read Draca stories?"

"And visit Dogon?" added Alita.

"Someone will, yes," said Faith. "I'm sure the council will send a wizard to read to Draca and protect her. But it won't be us. If the library closes, I'll be out of a job," said Faith.

"Will you be allowed to train me?" asked Kit. She

felt a huge lump forming in her throat. Her eyes were stinging.

"That's up to the Wizards' Council. But I think they'll probably make you wait until you're eighteen now."

"No!" cried Kit. "That's *forever*!"

Faith shook her head. "It might not come to that," she said. "I do have one last idea. But it's not for you to worry about."

"But . . . can't I help?" asked Kit. She was aware that her voice sounded whiny.

Faith shook her head irritably. "You're a very young, very new wizard. You need to leave this to me. It's not safe. I think it's time for you to get back to shelving."

"But what's the point, if the library is about to be knocked down?" Kit could feel her voice rising. She couldn't understand why Faith was treating her like a baby.

"That's enough!" Faith almost shouted. Purple sparks had started appearing at the edges of her eyes, which Kit knew wasn't a good sign.

"Go back to shelving now," the librarian continued, her voice more even.

"Come on, Kit," said Alita. Both she and Josh were
looking a bit nervously at Faith. But as the three
of them headed back through the stacks toward
the rest of the library, Kit couldn't stop thinking
about Salt and what would happen if he took over
the library the next day. How was she supposed to
just not worry about it? Was she supposed to have
a magic switch to turn off all her worries? That was
definitely not a spell Faith had taught her yet.

Was Faith ever going to teach her another spell
if Salt destroyed the library and she got fired? Did
Faith even care?

She didn't seem all that upset about the pros-
pect of giving up Kit's training. She just seemed
angry that Kit was in the way.

Maybe Faith wasn't actually that interested in
training Kit. Maybe she'd be relieved if she never
saw Kit again.

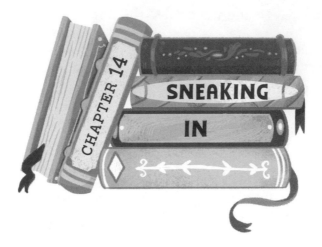

CHAPTER 14

SNEAKING IN

Josh and Alita started shelving as soon as they got back to the main library, but Kit couldn't concentrate.

Adults always thought they knew best. But Kit had imagined it would be different now that she was a wizard. She could do magic! But instead of doing something to help, she was just putting books on shelves and waiting to find out whether she would have to wait years to keep training.

Surely there was *something* she could do to stop Salt? Whatever Faith was doing, it hadn't done any good so far. She just expected Kit to trust her, but she wouldn't tell Kit anything. Would she have even told Kit about Draca if Kit hadn't followed her? And why was she waiting to stop Salt? If Kit were the one in charge, she wouldn't wait.

And what if Faith's plan, whatever it was, didn't work? Where would that leave Kit?

I've got this power, and I'm not allowed to use it. It's not fair!

Her frustration built and built until she couldn't wait anymore. She had to do something about Salt.

While Josh and Alita were still shelving, she marched back to the break room, which was now empty. She began looking through Faith's spell books. One book was sitting in front of the others— big and fat, with gold plating on the cover. It had no title, but there seemed to be all kinds of spells in there. There was a bookmark in it, on a page called SPELLS OF FORGETTING.

With her heart thumping, she picked it up. She could feel the power pulsing from it, the way she did with the books in the stacks. This was a powerful book. Dangerous.

It was perfect.

What if I make Salt forget all about the library? thought Kit. *What if I save the day?*

She decided to ignore the little inner voice reminding her that Faith had said mind magic was one of the most dangerous kinds.

And another little voice that pointed out that the last time she'd tried to do a spell on her own, she'd ended up being chased by a house on giant chicken legs.

Faith had said that anyone reading from a really powerful spell book could do magic. So surely a wizard doing it—the youngest wizard ever!—was bound to be even more powerful. It wouldn't be like with Baba Yaga's house. She wouldn't have any trouble remembering the spell—she'd just read it straight from the book.

And by the time she'd convinced herself she was doing the right thing, Kit had left the library and was walking down the street toward Salt's shiny office building and the penthouse at the very top.

CHAPTER 15

BREAKING IN

Kit knew that breaking and entering was wrong. She knew stealing Faith's book was wrong. But, she told herself, so was destroying the library. So doing this one little thing wrong was worth it to stop Salt.

Getting into Salt Enterprises was easy enough. It was just an ordinary office building. There was a guard at the front desk, but he was watching football on a little screen behind his desk. Kit slipped past him and down the corridor toward the elevator.

She pressed the button for the top floor. When

the elevator went *ding* at the top, she hurried out into the corridor and looked at all the doors for a sign saying which office was his.

In her bag was the book containing the spell. She just had to say it when he was in the room and he'd forget everything about the library. And they'd all be safe.

At the end of the hall there was a door with a plaque that read MR. SALT, CEO, MANAGING DIRECTOR, YOUR BOSS. She put her ear to the door, and, hearing no one inside, she carefully turned the handle. It was locked.

Oh, no! Kit thought. She glanced around and noticed there was a keypad next to the door. *There must be a code.*

She tried typing in 1-2-3-4-5-6, which was the password her dad used for everything.

The door didn't budge and made an angry beep at her.

Think, Kit, think. What would Salt use as a passcode? He's old, so he probably doesn't have a good one.

Wait. What did he say at the protest? It's his

birthday today. And what does Mom always use as her
password?

Kit keyed in the date . . . but what would the year
be? What year was Salt born?

It's his fiftieth birthday, so . . . hmm . . . what year
was it fifty years ago? That's it!

She put in the final numbers. A little green light
flashed, and there was a click.

The door was open.

Kit crept in, feeling very pleased with herself.
The office was huge. There was a massive gold-
framed portrait of Salt on one wall. On the opposite wall, there was another massive gold-framed
portrait of Salt. On the other two walls were even
larger gold-framed portraits of Salt. One of them
showed him standing on what looked like a dead
lion, holding a gun and grinning. Another showed
him bare-chested, riding a horse. The other two
showed him wrestling a bear and dressed as a king,
sitting on a throne.

He's modest, isn't he?

Kit glanced around for somewhere to hide and

spotted a door. It led to a bathroom—all gold and sparkling tiles, with even more pictures of Salt. This time they were framed photos of him with various celebrities. Kit wondered if all these celebrities knew they were watching Mr. Salt when he went to pee.

As she waited, she read over the spell in her head. She was careful not to say any of the words out loud in case she started the spell, but she wanted to make sure she didn't stumble when she said it. She didn't want to risk it going wrong and making *herself* forget what she was doing there.

After half an hour of waiting, Kit was starting to get very, very bored, when finally she heard footsteps and muffled voices. She couldn't hear quite what they were saying, so she touched her lips and whispered, *"Broadcast the quiet, ymhelaethu!"*

Now she could hear the voices as clearly as if they were in the bathroom with her. She was glad they weren't. Because what she heard made her suddenly very afraid.

"Tomorrow, Jenkins, we make our move," said Salt. "Tomorrow we wake the dragon and drain its power."

Oh, thought Kit. *OH.*

He knows about the dragon.

He knows about magic.

This is very, very bad.

"When I make myself High Wizard, I think I'll get a cloak made," Salt went on. "Purple and gold, do you think? I think I'd look very handsome in purple and gold. I hear that's what the Wizards' Council likes to wear."

"Sir, you're correct about the cloak, but I'm not sure there's such a thing as a High Wizard. From my research, there's a Wizards' Council, and I think the leader is called the Chairwizard."

"I don't care what those namby-pamby losers call their weak leaders. Things are going to change when I get my power from the dragon. You're sure that the Stone of Eek will be able to pull the power of the dragon into me?"

"Yes, sir, as long as you say the spell."

"Well, OBVIOUSLY I'm also going to say the spell. Don't be a complete and utter dunderhead, Jenkins. Honestly. It's a good thing I'm here to be the brains of this operation."

"Yes, sir," mumbled the man called Jenkins.

"Well, when I have my power, everything will be different. For a start, we're not going to have any of that government nonsense. I'll just be in charge of everything. I'm a great businessman. I'll be great at running other things, too. Prisons. Schools. They're the same thing, aren't they?"

This was terrible! Salt didn't want to buy the library to build a shopping center.

He wants to wake the dragon!

"What are you going to do first?" asked Jenkins.

"I'd tell you if you didn't keep interrupting me,

you feeble dweeb. The first thing I'm going to do is turn all the people who wronged me into toads. Newts. Slimy animals. Maybe snakes?"

A man who thinks that snakes are actually slimy is going to try to wake up the dragon, thought Kit. *I have to stop him* now!

"Jenkins, is the Stone of Eek ready? Do you have the spell for me to read?"

"It's all ready, sir."

"Then leave me. I want to plot the downfall of all the people who've ever insulted me. I think I'll start with the girl who wouldn't go with me to the school dance back in nineteen seventy-nine. Kimberly Jones, you're first on my list . . ."

Kit heard the door to Salt's office open and close as Jenkins left. Salt was alone. This was her chance. It was now or never.

Kit started to read the forgetting spell as quietly as she could. It was longer than anything she'd attempted so far. It was the first spell she'd read out loud from a book. She hoped there weren't any gestures she was supposed to be doing.

She was almost at the end when, suddenly, the door opened.

She was crouched on the floor, clutching the book and looking up at Salt.

"A child spy in my private bathroom!" said Salt. "Who sent you?"

"No one," said Kit truthfully. "I sent myself."

Salt grabbed her by the wrist and hauled her to her feet, snatching the book out of her hands.

He looked at it with a puzzled expression and then yelled, "JENKINS!"

Jenkins scuttled into the room. He stared at Kit. But Salt didn't seem interested in providing explanations. "What does this book say?"

He thrust the book at Jenkins, who looked over the spell. "It's a forgetting spell, sir. A powerful one, I think, based on everything I've read about magic."

Salt's pink face turned purple with rage. "WHAT? This little snot was trying to make me forget—" He broke off, looking down at Kit. He was still gripping her wrist. It hurt a lot. "What were you trying to make me forget?"

"Your wife's birthday. So she'd be angry with you. And that would serve you right," said Kit.

"Nice try," said Salt. "I divorced my ninth wife last week." He turned to Jenkins. "What's she REALLY doing?"

"Well . . ." said Jenkins. He furrowed his brow. "I imagine . . . she was probably trying to make you forget about the dragon?"

"That's what I was going to say before you SO RUDELY INTERRUPTED ME!" yelled Salt. "Get out! And take this little piece of child-shaped nonsense to the police!"

Jenkins took her, slightly more gently, by the arm. "You'd better come with me," he hissed. "Don't make Mr. Salt even angrier than he already is."

"I'll keep the book. Thank you," said Salt. "This will be useful to stop you all from coming after me once I've woken the dragon. You can't use the spells if you don't have the book."

"It won't matter. If you wake the dragon, it'll kill everyone," said Kit.

"Don't be ridiculous. I'll be the most powerful

wizard in the world. I'll be able to control the dragon. I'm intelligent, talented, strong-willed . . . I'll make better use of the dragon than your pathetic bunch of sniveling *librarians*!" He spat the last word. "Such a waste of all that power. Well, don't worry. I'll do the best things with it. I'll create the best spells. I'll rule the world like it's never been ruled before."

There was a sudden flash and a frizzle of electricity.

Faith was standing beside them. With a single movement, she snatched the book from Salt. "I'll take that."

Her eyes glowed from within, tinged with purple instead of their usual deep black-brown.

Salt looked terrified. "Don't hurt me!" he cried. "I'll call security!"

"But when they get here, you won't remember why you called them," said Faith. And she began to recite the rest of the spell that Kit had begun. She spoke quickly, her eyes glowing a bright, flickering violet as the spell took effect.

When she was finished, Salt was staring blankly into the middle distance. So was Jenkins.

"Quick. Let's go." Faith took Kit's hand, holding the book in the other. "They'll snap out of it in a minute." She raised a hand and made a complicated movement, whispering, *"Telay!"*

And they both vanished.

A moment later, they were standing in the stacks. Josh, Alita, and Dogon were waiting for them.

"Kit! You're OK!" said Alita, rushing toward Kit, her thick black braids flying out behind her. She threw her arms around her friend in a tight hug. Dogon flew up to lick her face with his rough tongue.

"What happened?" asked Josh. "Faith sensed that a powerful spell was happening nearby."

Kit couldn't meet their eyes.

"Kit has done something very dangerous," said Faith. "She attempted a spell on Salt that I was going to use to stop him. Without permission. Without thinking about the consequences."

Kit felt her face get hot. "I . . . wanted to help," she said. Then, looking up angrily, she said, "You weren't *doing* anything. He was about to wake up the dragon! He said he was going to do it tomorrow! And you were just waiting around and not doing anything."

"No," said Faith icily. She waved the book at Kit. "I was going to cast a forgetting spell on him *tomorrow*, before he began his own spell. He was going to forget all about waking the dragon. All our problems would have been solved."

"You *knew* he was going to wake the dragon?" asked Kit.

Faith gave a brief nod. "I've been doing my own investigations. And I learned the Stone of Eek was missing from the National Museum of Magic."

"There's a museum of magic?" Josh's eyes lit up. "I mean . . . I'll ask about that later. Go on."

"Who stole it?" asked Kit.

"It could've been any of the shadier magical traders," said Faith. "But what put me on the right trail was that I heard someone had paid rather a lot of money for it at the Black Market—and for the spell that goes with it, to wake the dragon—and that the person who paid the money was called Jenkins. Who happens to work for Hadrian Salt. So I put two and two together and came up with Almost-Certain Apocalypse."

Kit couldn't believe this. "Why didn't you *tell* me?"

"You're ten years old," said Faith. "I didn't want to scare you."

"Are you saying I'm a coward?" asked Kit.

Faith shook her head. "No. I just . . . You shouldn't have to worry about the end of the world at your age. You should be playing with your friends. Learning easy spells. Reading books. Being a child."

"That's not fair," said Kit. "I wasn't worried about the end of the world, but I was worried about not being able to carry on with my training. I just got my powers. There's finally something special about me—and you didn't even care that it might get taken away. You didn't care if you never saw me again."

Faith looked horrified. "Kit. That's not true. Of course I cared."

But Kit couldn't stop. "You've been keeping things from me from the start. You probably wouldn't have told me about Draca if I hadn't followed you. You keep telling me what to do, but you never give me a reason! I'm a wizard, like you. You could have told me you were working on a spell, you could have told me your plan, and then I wouldn't have had to worry. But it doesn't matter. The forgetting spell is done now. By a *wizard*." She gave Faith a defiant look. "So I saved everyone a day early."

Faith pinched the bridge of her nose. She didn't look angry anymore, just defeated. "No, Kit, you didn't. You don't understand. You performed the spell that I have been preparing, drawing more of the dragon's power into the book every day. But you used it up before it was ready. Now he'll just forget the last few hours—and we're left without a spell to stop him."

Kit felt the words stab her like a spear of ice right through the ribs. "Oh." She tried to rally. "You didn't have to *finish* the spell I started if you knew all that. Why did you finish it and use it all up?"

"Because with a spell that powerful, you can't just stop halfway through," said Faith, her voice rising and tiny glints of purple appearing at the edges of her eyes. "The magic must be completed or it will go wild. And wild magic, roaming loose in the world, is . . . Let's just say *bad*."

"Oh." Kit winced. It was all her fault.

The librarian took a deep breath and sighed. All her anger seemed to fade away. She suddenly looked very sad. "Perhaps I should've told you what I was doing. But I've never had an apprentice before. I don't know how much you can cope with. You're still very young, Kit. As you showed by going off like that and doing something so foolish!"

Kit hung her head. Now, if the world ended, it was going to be because of her.

"Well, it's done now. You should all go home and rest. We'll meet tomorrow and see if we can fix your mess, Kit."

Kit walked home with Alita and Josh in silence. She felt the guilt and shame like a stone in her chest. She couldn't stop thinking about what would happen if the dragon woke up. Her family, her school, Alita and Josh—all gone. Because of her.

"I have to do something to stop Salt," she said finally as they approached her house.

The others stopped walking. "No, Kit, don't you *get* it?" said Alita. "Doing stuff on your own is what got us into this mess." She looked at Kit out of the corner of her eye. "You should have told us what you were planning."

"Then we would have told you not to do it," said Josh.

"Maybe you're right." Kit sighed. "You'd both be better wizards than me. You're smarter. You like books. You don't go off and do careless things. I don't even get why I have these powers. What a waste. No matter what I do, it goes wrong."

Kit felt a tickle at the back of her throat and blinked her eyes hard. She was not going to cry. Kit Spencer never cried. But it was so unfair. She'd thought there was finally something special about her. But it turned out her special power was destroying the world.

There was silence. Kit couldn't meet her friends' eyes. Maybe they hated her now. Maybe she'd done something so bad they couldn't forgive her.

But Josh said, "Maybe a few things went wrong when you tried to do them on your own. So you shouldn't do something on your own. *We* should do something. Together."

"Even if you are a total disaster," added Alita. She gave Kit the smallest smile.

That made Kit feel ever so slightly better.

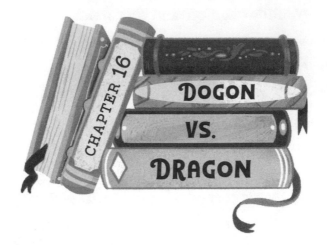

CHAPTER 16

DOGON VS. DRAGON

The time had come. Moments after Kit, Josh, and Alita arrived at the library, before they'd even had a chance to say hello to Faith, Salt strode in, surrounded by men in suits.

"Excellent," he said. "This is all mine. You have to leave now."

"We still have to move the books," protested Faith.

"Nope. Mine now. I bought everything that belongs to the public library," said Salt. "You need to leave."

Faith blinked. She turned to the children and

said, "Come and help me collect my things." She gave them a meaningful look. "My personal collection."

Kit, Josh, and Alita followed her, unsure what she might be talking about. She headed for the shelves at the back of the library, behind the sliding glass panel.

The portal books! thought Kit. They went to help her carry them. There was a book about making your own jam, the garden book, a comic book about Romans . . . Soon they had the full collection. Almost.

"Kit, get the first one you used," said Faith.

The dangerous animals book, Kit realized. She scanned the shelves for it. Where had she put it? She was definitely supposed to reshelve it the other day.

"What are we doing with these?" whispered Alita. "And when are we going to collect Dogon? We can't leave him here. And what about the dragon?"

"Shh!" said Faith. "Have we got all the books?"

Kit was busy looking at Salt as he paced up and down. Her eyes followed him. "How are we going to beat him?" she murmured to herself.

"Right!" Faith said loudly. "Let's go and get my handbag. Then we can go."

She led them down to the stacks, where they picked up Dogon. He perched on Alita's shoulder, looking worried and making a growling sound in the back of his throat.

They could hear Salt barking orders above in the library. "It's just garbage. We don't need any of it. Put it in the dumpster."

They shuddered. "He's going to throw the books away!" said Josh.

"We can rescue them from the dumpster later," said Faith.

"What about the book forest?" asked Alita. "It's Dogon's home!"

"I have to think," said Faith. "First let's store these books."

She propped the garden book up on the branch of a tree and started to read it, holding the other books in her arms, then disappeared. When she reappeared, she wasn't carrying anything. "Those books will be safe in the garden for now. Though we shouldn't leave them for too long or they'll get damp. Now we need to go and get help."

"Where are we going?" asked Alita.

"Good question. I haven't thought that far ahead," said Faith. "I have to admit, I didn't think Salt would be the sort to get up so early in the morning. I thought we'd have more time."

"How about my house? There are always so many people there, I doubt my parents would mind a few more. Or even notice."

"Thanks, Kit, that would be great," said Faith, giving her a little smile.

"Dogon will need to hide," said Alita.

"Yeah, I don't think even my parents would be very happy to have a magical fire-breathing dog as a houseguest," said Kit.

So they traipsed to Kit's house, with Dogon hidden in a cloth bag. Alita gave him strict instructions to be very, very quiet and not breathe fire.

Kit put her key in the lock and peered inside. The coast was clear. She could hear Baby crying upstairs. A second later, Toddler started yelling.

"I think my parents will be busy for a while," Kit said.

"I think Dogon really wants to get out," whispered Alita. The duffel bag was starting to float and flap around.

They headed into the kitchen. Dogon popped out of the duffel bag and flew out onto Alita's shoulder. He made a purring sound and nuzzled into her neck.

Faith turned to them with a very serious expression. Kit didn't like it one bit.

"I've got something to tell you," she said. "I spoke to the Wizards' Council earlier."

"Are they angry?" asked Kit. "That I wasted the spell?"

Faith's mouth was set in a thin line. "You know how angry I was when I found out you'd stolen my spell book to use it on Salt?"

Kit nodded.

"Multiply that by ten and add the bad tempers of old men and women who think anyone under eighty is a whippersnapper. Then multiply that by the biggest number you can imagine. And that's still only about half as angry as they are."

Kit gulped. This was her fault. "Can't you blame it all on me? I was the one who wasted your big spell."

Faith shook her head firmly. "You're my responsibility. I'm the grown-up here." She smiled. "Even though I sometimes feel like I'm making it all up as I go along."

"Grown-ups feel like that, too?" asked Alita in shock.

"Grown-ups have *feelings*?" asked Josh. He looked at Faith, blinking.

"Yes, grown-ups have feelings," said Faith. "You don't stop being human when you turn eighteen, you know. You still get scared and unsure. Quite often, actually."

"Well," said Kit, who thought that was quite enough talking about feelings. "What did the Wizards' Council say we should do?"

"They said they would handle it. They told me—very firmly—that they'll take it from here." She gave a heavy sigh. "I'm worried they might stop you from using magic entirely after this."

Kit wanted to cry. If she was banned from using magic, she'd just be the same average, muddy, in-the-way Kit she'd always been.

"Actually," said Faith, "they might not stop *you* from doing magic. They might stop me instead. This happened on my watch. They told me to handle things, and I let this happen."

"No!" said Kit. "That's not fair."

"Fair isn't really how secret magical organizations roll," said Faith glumly.

"So we're just going to sit here and wait for the council to handle things? And even if they beat Salt, they'll probably stop us from doing magic?" asked Kit in horror.

"No," said Faith. "We're not going to wait. We're going to disobey them and take matters into our own hands."

"Isn't that the exact same thing you got angry at me for doing?" asked Kit.

"Yes. But now I'm doing it. I've been rebelling

against the council *far* longer than you have." Faith gave her a grin.

"Well, if we're going to break the rules, we should at least be logical about it," said Josh. "What's our problem? That Salt is going to wake up the dragon, right? So we need to find a way to stop him from waking the dragon. Is there some kind of . . . anti-waking-up spell?" suggested Josh.

"Nothing that we could use without harming the dragon," said Faith. "We could end up putting the poor beast in a coma."

"Wait," said Alita. "Could we persuade Salt that he doesn't *want* to do it in the first place? What makes people *not* want to do things?"

"When things are terrible," said Kit. "No one wants to wield something useless. We could tell him the dragon doesn't work. Say it's broken."

"He wouldn't fall for that," said Josh.

"We could say it's dead?" said Kit.

"What, and put a fake dead dragon there?" said Josh. "Where are we going to get a fake dead dragon?"

"Magic, obviously," said Kit. She looked at Faith. "Can we?"

Faith was looking thoughtful. "Yes. I mean, you could, but he might get too close to a dead dragon, and it would break the illusion. Knowing Salt, he'd probably go and kick the thing to make sure it was dead."

"How about the illusion of a live dragon, then?" asked Kit. "That might scare him off. Is there a fake dragon spell I could do?"

"Hmm, well. Yes," said Faith. "But we'd need something to build the spell around. Just like a convincing lie has a bit of truth at the middle to make it convincing, we'd need something to use as the base of the dragon."

"Dogon!" said Alita. Dogon fluttered up into the air in surprise at hearing his name, letting out a snort of smoke. She gave him a reassuring pat, and then he took off and flew around the kitchen.

"Dogon's part dragon," Alita went on. "So you're partway there already, even before the illusion!"

"Excellent," said Faith. Her face fell. "Except

he'll need to stay still. Dogon *never* stays still."

"He will if I tell him to," said Alita. "We understand each other."

Dogon peeked his head out of the snack cupboard. He had crumbs all around his muzzle.

"Bad Dogon. Down!" said Alita.

Dogon fluttered down to the floor and sat obediently at her feet.

Faith frowned. "He's never that good for me. You've got something there, Alita. A career in dragon taming?"

Alita's eyes lit up. "Is that a real job?"

"It is. Although you might need to keep your hair a bit shorter," said Faith, gesturing at Alita's two long braids. "The smell of burning hair is really not very nice."

"How good is the illusion going to be, though?" said Josh. He looked doubtfully at Dogon's furry, crumb-covered face.

"Very," said Faith. "But it won't work to the touch. Salt can't come too close."

"Can't you add fire? Then he won't *want* to come

too close," suggested Kit. "How about an elemental fire spell? I can do that! Watch!"

Kit muttered her fire spell, and a huge fireball emerged from her fingers. Everyone threw themselves to the ground. Thankfully the kitchen window was open, and the fireball sailed out into the garden instead of burning the house down.

Kit's mom called downstairs from the baby's room, "You're not breaking things down there, are you, Kit?"

"No, Mom!" she called back.

When they'd gotten up and dusted themselves off, Faith cleared her throat.

"You can do the illusion spell, Kit. I'll handle the fire spell. I like my face, and I don't want it melted off."

Kit grumbled. "That was bad luck, that fireball. I bet I could do it next time." But she did see Faith's point. Maybe she needed *slightly* more practice with the fire spells before going into battle with them.

"But there's another thing. We need to get into the library unnoticed," said Faith. "We'll need time to set all this up without Salt knowing about it. Perhaps I could create a distraction. Although that could attract public attention that we don't want, of course."

"Couldn't we use a portal book to get into the library?" asked Josh.

Faith shook her head. "We took all the portal books out of the library," she said. "You gathered them all up."

Kit blushed. "Actually, I think I forgot one."

"Kit!" said Josh.

"No, this could be a good thing," said Faith. "Which one?"

"*Dangerous Animals*," said Kit. "I was looking for it—oh, I just remembered where it is! I left it down in the stacks. I was supposed to reshelve it . . . Anyway, I was looking for it when we were leaving, but I got distracted and, well, it's still in the stacks."

Kit braced herself, but Faith laughed. "Oh, Kit! I'm not angry. You've left us a door!" She gave Kit a long, measured look. "I think wild magic chose well when it picked you. Sometimes a little chaos, a little wildness, can be an advantage."

Kit felt a smile spreading across her face.

Josh, however, was frowning. "But how does it help us if Kit left the book behind? That's not a door on its own. We need a second copy of *Dangerous Animals* that's outside the library to use as a portal, right?"

"That's right," said Faith. "Clever boy. And I know someone who has one." She gestured to the garden book. "We can use this to get to their library, then use *their* copy of *Dangerous Animals* to get us into our library. Now, Kit, do you think your parents might have some meat in the fridge?"

Before they left, they made sure they had every detail of their plan worked out. Everyone had a part to play, and everyone had to play it well, or Salt might guess he was being fooled.

Once they'd decided exactly who was doing what and how, Faith opened the garden book. "Link hands, everyone."

"Dogon, on my shoulder!" instructed Alita. The little creature flapped his way up and perched, nuzzling into Alita's neck.

Faith began to read.

A moment later, they appeared inside the garden book.

"I've only ever popped out the other side of a book by accident," said Kit. "How do we get to the other library?"

"For a start, we walk," said Faith. "Then there's another spell at the other end."

So they walked through the first garden. It looked a little different than the last time Kit had visited. Smaller, somehow.

"It's not how I remember," said Kit.

"It never quite is. Each time a person steps into one of these books, the world is different. Especially because this time I read the book out loud," said Faith. "So this is my reading. I always remember the rosebushes."

They came close to a cluster of rosebushes and turned a corner. There was a brick wall and, in it, a door. They walked through it and came into a new garden—Kit recognized it. It was the picture on the second page.

"So each garden is a page?"

"Two pages," said Faith. "Each garden is two pages in the book."

They walked through thirty or forty more gardens—Kit lost count—of all kinds.

"I'm glad this book isn't longer," said Kit. "I'm exhausted!

"Yes, that's why people hardly ever use portal books longer than fifty pages. You *can* enter on a later page, but that can have unfortunate side effects."

"Like what?" asked Josh.

"Sometimes the pages you skip get annoyed and bleed through into the real world. Which is fine if it

means a bit of moss growing in the library, but you wouldn't want a black mamba loose in nonfiction, would you?"

Kit, remembering the creature's beady eyes and angry hiss, shook her head very firmly.

Eventually they reached a tall, thick hedge, wound all through with flowers and thorns.

"This is the final page," said Faith.

"How do we get out?" asked Alita.

"You need to cast a spell to go to the library you want. You say the library's name, then the same spell you always use to leave a book. *Morningside, hus!*" said Faith.

They appeared in the corner of a library in front of a row of books. A small, curly-haired girl was staring at them. Her mouth dropped open.

"Ah," said Faith. "This is awkward."

The girl was still staring. Faith knelt down. "Would you like to see a puppy?"

The little girl nodded.

Faith made a gesture and said, *"Chien see, chien be!"*

At once, the little girl's face lost its look of terror and she beamed, then trotted away.

"Where are we?" asked Alita. She peered after the child. "Are there puppies here?"

"No puppies," Faith whispered, in case the girl was still within earshot. "That was just an illusion spell to make that child think she saw a puppy instead of a gang of strangers appearing from a book. Illusion spells work very well on young children, as their sense of what's real and what isn't is blurry at the best of times."

"Now, what we came for." Faith strode over to a wooden cabinet on one wall of the library, looked around, gestured a spell to open it, and rifled through the shelves inside until she found the dangerous animals book.

"I'm going to have to apologize profusely to Gerald later," she said. "He's the librarian here—we're not supposed to show up and use the portal books without asking. He'll understand, though. It's an apocalypse. Apocalypse rules are different.

Are you ready, Kit? We'll need a cold spell for the first page. Cold makes reptiles sleepy."

"Ready," said Kit.

Josh propped the dangerous animals book up on a shelf, and they checked that there was no one around.

Faith began to read from the book.

When they appeared in the desert, they were ready. Kit and Faith chanted an elemental spell together.

Dylai fod yn oer,
The cold is in your bones,
Tu kulir irukka ventum,
Einfrieren!

Instead of striking, the snake from before curled up, looking sleepy. It was almost cute, curled into a coil like that.

"One down," said Faith. "Come on."

They had been walking for nearly ten minutes when the desert began to turn into a jungle.

"It's a tiger next," said Faith. "But it's OK. The page starts by talking about tiger cubs, so just throw this at them and we'll be fine . . . if we run."

She handed out raw meat from a plastic bag in her pocket. The pocket never seemed to be full but always had so many objects in it. Kit made a mental note to ask her about that sometime.

GROWWWWWWWL.

Tiger cubs came tumbling out from among the trees. Their claws and teeth looked very sharp, but they were still adorable. One of them tripped over its big furry paws as it stalked toward them.

"Throw the meat now!" said Faith.

They chucked the pieces of meat at the cubs, who fell on the food hungrily, growling and purring with pleasure.

They ran through the trees.

It was hot. The air felt like soup. But Kit ran like her life depended on it.

Next came a herd of charging rhinos. With a bark and a roar, Dogon dive-bombed the lead rhino, and the herd changed course.

After that, by a river, where flies buzzed and bothered them as they walked, they came across a snapping crocodile. It ran toward them, belly low to the ground, and Kit let out a little squeak of fear. But before the crocodile was within ten feet of them, Faith produced some chewing gum from her pocket and, with a muttered spell, grew it into a sticky net and bound the beast's jaws shut.

"Shame," said Faith. "That was my last piece of gum. It was cinnamon flavor, too!"

They walked on and on, facing poisonous frogs and a river full of razor-toothed piranhas. To get past the frogs, Faith cast a protection spell that created a thin coating of an invisible rubber-like substance all over their bodies, repelling the frog poison. The piranhas turned out to be the easiest creatures to get past—Faith simply created a glowing magical bridge across their river, and the children walked safely over, far above the snapping jaws of the hungry fish.

And at last they came to the end of the book. A thick wall of jungle stretched from the ground right up into the sky and across their path, as far as they could see.

"Right," said Faith. "Let's go."

But Kit heard a noise behind them. A horrible noise, like the hooting of a monstrous owl. She whipped around.

"Faith, look."

The others all turned to face what Kit was seeing.

"I can't be totally sure," said Josh in a terrified whisper. "But I think we might be being attacked by aliens."

"Oh," said Faith. "This isn't good. It means wild magic is being released. It's making the books leak. Salt must have started the spell!"

"But how are the aliens—"

"I'll explain more later. When we've definitely survived," said Faith.

Facing them was a row of octopus-like creatures, each with a beak-like mouth and a tangle of tentacles emerging from their slimy heads. They were making horrible hooting sounds.

Kit saw a flashing light and felt a blast of heat right by her cheek. She flinched, bumping into Alita, who hugged her close.

"We're being attacked by aliens armed with lasers!" yelled Josh. "If I weren't terrified, this would be *awesome!*"

Faith was muttering something, cupping her hands together, then spreading them out.

There was a *whoosh* of air and a bright flash, and suddenly the aliens sounded very far away.

"Shield spell," explained Faith. "It'll hold them off for now. You have to go! There isn't much time. Stop Salt without me. I have to stop these—"

"Aliens," said Josh helpfully.

Kit felt a well of panic in her stomach. "But you said I couldn't . . . that I'd do the fireball spell wrong," said Kit. "What if I blow up the library?"

Faith looked at her, still holding her hands up to maintain the shield. Alien laser blasts were pinging off the outside. Kit thought she heard a slight tearing sound . . .

"You can do this, Kit. The illusion will

remain for a few minutes without you doing anything, so you can shoot off the odd fireball. You
can do anything if you try," said Faith. She looked
around at the others. "You all know your jobs. Now
go! Say the home spell!"

"*Hus!*" said Kit.

And they appeared in the woods beneath the
library, beside a book cart that Kit had left behind
with the dangerous animals book on it.

They could hear a loud, droning male voice above
them, coming from the center of the library. Salt
was beginning his spell.

"We don't have much time," whispered Kit.

CHAPTER 17

SALT, HEAD OF THE LIBRARY

Salt was standing in the library. He felt tingly all over. He was also feeling very sweaty. Doing magic was hard work.

"I think it's working, Jenkins," said Salt. He'd only spoken a few lines of the spell, but he could already hear rumbling beneath him. Power surged through his body. "It's working!"

"Yes, sir," said Jenkins, who was holding the spell book open while Salt read. They were in the center of the library, beneath the skylight. Salt held the Stone of Eek in his hand. Was it his imagination, or was it starting to glow?

He read on.

"On wanre nicht kam draconis,
Issy macht die wak . . ."

A rumbling sound was building beneath the library. Smoke was wafting in between the shelves, as though someone were burning a fire nearby.

Salt felt a deep throbbing beneath his feet.

"Are you sure about this, sir?" asked Jenkins. "Waking the dragon, I mean? What if it's angry when it wakes up?"

"Do I want to wake the dragon?" scoffed Salt. "Do I want to become a powerful wizard and rule the world? What a ridiculous question. Now, turn the page."

Jenkins swallowed and blinked, then turned the page. Salt read a sentence or two more. The rumbling sound grew.

"Sir," came a young voice. "I am here to help you."

Salt stopped reading. Jenkins dropped the book in surprise.

A small, dark-haired, brown-skinned girl with her hair in long braids appeared from between two shelves, dressed in long flowing robes. "You are the head of the library," she said. Her face was serious and very intense. "The dragon sent me to you."

Salt puffed out his chest. "Head of the library today—tomorrow, the world!" He turned to Jenkins. "Did you know she'd appear?"

Jenkins shook his head. "No. But the man who sold me the book didn't tell me much. Just that you have to hold the stone and read the spell."

"The spell summoned me. I have come to take you to the dragon," said the girl. "I am the high priestess of this library. I serve the dragon. She came to me in a dream. She told me that you were too powerful and in possession of the Stone of Eek, and so she decided it was best that I brought you to her, so that you could wake her more peacefully. Without danger. She surrenders."

"I should think so, too!" Salt raised an eyebrow. "But . . . a little girl? A high priestess? That's not very impressive. High priestesses should be tall and imposing and at least eighteen years old."

"The old one got eaten," said the little girl. "The dragon does that sometimes."

Salt gulped.

"Come," said the little girl. "Do you have the Stone of Eek?"

"Of course. I keep it with me always." He held out the stone. "Can't have it falling into the wrong hands."

"That's sensible," said the little girl. "There are some bad people out there. Now, it's time to go."

The little girl led him and Jenkins to a bookcase and pulled out one of the books. Salt could've sworn he heard a whisper from behind the shelves. Then the bookcase began to revolve, and the little girl beckoned them inside.

"I must get one of these for my office!" said Salt. "That would impress people a lot. Although perhaps once I'm a powerful wizard, I can just program their minds to worship me. That would save all the trouble of actually having to do impressive things."

"Hush," said the high priestess. "You don't want to wake the dragon before you use the stone, or she will eat you."

Salt shut up. Possibly for the first time in his life.

They walked down a dark corridor, emerging into a forest. Salt couldn't believe his eyes.

He hated forests. They had no towers, no fluorescent lights, no cars . . . nothing of interest to him at all. But he could soon bulldoze this one. That could wait.

"Where's the dragon?" he asked.

The high priestess put a finger to her lips and pointed. Ahead, between the trees, was a glittering shape. They walked closer . . . and he realized it was a dragon.

There was something oddly furry about it. But it was definitely a dragon. It started to move, flapping its wings, although its eyes were closed. A puff of smoke emerged from its nostrils.

"Good dog! Stay!" said the high priestess.

"Did you just say 'good dog'?" asked Jenkins.

"No," said the high priestess. "I definitely didn't. You misheard. I said 'dragon.'"

The high priestess looked nervous. Salt assumed it must be because she was about to wake the dragon.

"I will now begin the spell," said the high priestess. "You must hold the stone. That will transfer the dragon's power to you."

Salt clutched it so hard his knuckles went white. He couldn't wait. He could imagine the power flowing into him, making him the most powerful man in the universe. Enabling him to do whatever he wanted without pesky human laws getting in the way.

The high priestess began to murmur words in a strange language. A spell, perhaps?

Salt held the stone and waited for the dragon to wake . . .

There was a rumbling sound. The dragon's eyelids began to flutter. Its eyes blinked open. It rose up and roared. Fire burst forth from its jaws, and Salt leaped out of the way, falling on his bottom.

"I HAVE AWOKEN!" came a booming voice. "I AM THE DRAGON. WHO DARES DISTURB MY REST?"

"S-S-Salt. My name is Salt. But you can call me . . . Master," said Salt.

The dragon smiled, showing glinting teeth. "I WILL CALL YOU NOTHING OF THE KIND, MORTAL. I WILL CALL YOU DINNER."

"What?" Salt stepped back. He looked at the high priestess . . . but she was gone.

"YOU HAVE BEEN TRICKED. MY PRIESTESS BROUGHT YOU TO WAKE ME, FOR NO WIZARD WOULD EVER DARE . . . BECAUSE NOW I AM FREE!"

"But . . . the stone?" said Salt. "In all the books Jenkins found, it said it would drain your power and give it to the person who held it!"

"DON'T BELIEVE EVERYTHING YOU READ," boomed the dragon.

"Well, I don't accept this! JENKINS! I need another spell."

Jenkins started leafing through the heavy spell book.

"Uh . . . " said the dragon, sounding ever-so-slightly uncertain. "RUN, MORTAL! OR FACE MY WRATH! RUN AND NEVER RETURN!"

The dragon breathed out an enormous fireball. It shot across the top of Salt's head, singeing his hair.

"Eeeek!" shrieked Salt, swatting at his head to put out the fire. But he stood his ground. He wasn't going to let this dragon win, even if he couldn't have its power. "I need a spell to crush this dragon! NOW, Jenkins!"

"What about this one?" asked Jenkins. "It creates an explosion that the spell-caster is protected from. Or this one that turns bones into dust. Or there's one called 'Evil Begone'—the description says it's a spell to defeat evildoers. That should cover dragons, shouldn't it? Apparently it makes them so afraid, they run away and never come back."

Salt could have sworn he heard small, childish voices whispering from behind the trees. Then the dragon boomed out.

"WHATEVER YOU DO, PLEASE DON'T USE THE EVIL BEGONE SPELL. THAT ONE IS

PARTICULARLY PAINFUL FOR DRAGONS."

"HA!" crowed Salt. "Then that's exactly the spell we'll do. You pathetic giant lizard, you've sealed your own fate!"

Jenkins passed him the book, and he began to read. He was relieved to see that it was in English, for once.

"Evil, begone. Evil, flee.
Evil, feast on fear and fly!
The one whose heart is full of hate,
BEGONE! If you do not, you'll die!"

As soon as he had finished, Salt suddenly felt a wave of terror wash over him. He'd never been more afraid in his entire life. He felt an urge to run. An urge to scream.

He did both. Jenkins was just behind him. They ran and ran and screamed and screamed, through the woods, up the dark tunnel, until they were back in the library, then back out on the street, then halfway down the road. They ran until they were panting for breath. They ran until their legs felt like jelly and they couldn't walk, never mind run.

"What do we do now, sir?" gasped Jenkins. "I feel this enormous urge to keep running."

"We're leaving. Pack everything up! We're going to build a shopping center very, very, very far away from here."

"But what about the dragon?" said Jenkins.

"We're never going to mention it again, you hear me? There are no dragons. Dragons don't exist. I'm a businessman. I do business. I don't fuss around with mythical creatures. That's for little kids and girls. OK? Got it?"

Jenkins nodded enthusiastically.

Salt wasn't sure why his spell against the evil dragon hadn't worked, but he knew that he never wanted to be anywhere near that terrifying library or that horrifying beast again.

CHAPTER 18

TEA AND TOMORROW

Down in the stacks, Kit exhaled. She was standing behind a tree, and her brain hurt. Keeping the dragon illusion spell going for so long had been very hard—especially since she had to alternate it with creating fireballs. She wanted to dunk her head in a bath of cold water. She shook away some of the feeling.

The illusion was fading. Dogon was sitting in the clearing, looking confused. Alita, still in her high priestess robes, came and fussed over him, stroking his fur and murmuring, "Good Dogon! Good Dogon!"

"That was great, Alita!" said Kit.

Alita blushed. "Thanks. I added a spell from Danny Fandango, just to make it more convincing."

"I *thought* I recognized it!" said Josh. He came out from behind the tree where he'd been hiding and coughed. "That dragon voice was hard to keep up. I think I need to gargle."

"It was very good, though," said Kit.

"So was your dragon illusion!" said Josh.

"And I think we can all agree that the fireballs were amazing, and no one got their face melted off even a bit," said Faith, stepping out from behind a tree.

"Faith! How long have you been there?" asked Kit.

"Just long enough to see how well you all did." She smiled. "When Salt didn't run away from the dragon illusion, I almost stepped in. But then I heard you three whispering, and suddenly you were persuading Salt to use the one spell in the book that would backfire on him!"

"That was Kit's idea," said Alita.

Kit grinned. "Salt didn't think for a second that *he* might be the evildoer in the room."

"Evil people do tend to think they're the heroes of their own stories," said Faith. "Well done, all three of you."

"Four!" said Alita, stroking Dogon, who was looking sleepy and dazed but perfectly content.

"So . . . we've saved the library?" asked Kit.

"And the world?" asked Josh hopefully. "Just like Danny Fandango?"

"Just like Lara Fandango, you mean?" said Alita.

"Just like all the heroes in all the books," said Faith.

Kit sighed with relief. She felt like she'd been holding her breath for hours. Maybe days.

"Speaking of books," said Josh, "why were those aliens in the dangerous animals book? They were aliens, right? From another book?"

Faith nodded. "Martians, in fact. Or rather, in fiction. They were from a book called *The War of the Worlds*, by H. G. Wells. The wild magic released by Salt's spell was making the books bleed together.

We're lucky it wasn't something even *more* dangerous that got into our book."

"How did you fight them off?" asked Kit. "The aliens, I mean. Did you kill them?"

"No. I can't risk damaging the books by killing their characters off," said Faith. "But I remembered that they don't have any immunity to Earth diseases. So"—she grinned—"I pretended I was going to sneeze, and they ran away long enough for me to escape back to the library."

Kit giggled. "So you defeated the aliens with . . . snot?"

"Imaginary snot," giggled Alita.

Faith was shaking her head and smiling at them. "Well," she said, "I think there's time for a cup of ginger tea before you go back home. I have some coconut squares, too. I imagine your parents might be expecting you home soon. I have to call the Wizards' Council. They should have sensed that the dragon has settled by now, but just in case they're about to do a powerful spell for no reason, I should let them know!"

"Can I meet them soon?" asked Kit.

"Soon," said Faith. "But in the meantime, I have a lot of tidying up to do. Hopefully Greg has picked all the books out of the dumpster by now. Then tomorrow, back for more training?"

The children nodded.

CHAPTER 19

READING A BOOK ON PURPOSE

When Kit got home, her mother was still busy with Baby. Josh and Alita said a quick goodbye, then hurried off home.

The world was saved. And Baby was being noisily sick.

Just then Kit's brother and sister came in through the front door, arguing.

"You're not going to tell Mom," said Wicked Older Brother.

"What's in it for me?" said Perfect Older Sister.

"I could promise not to take your favorite—" began Wicked.

They both stopped when they saw Kit in the kitchen, holding the garden book.

"Wait . . . Kit . . . are you *reading*?" asked Wicked.

"A book? On purpose?" asked Perfect Older Sister.

They both shook their heads.

"Something weird is going on," said Wicked.

Kit shrugged innocently. "Just reading. No big deal."

But that was a lie. She'd just saved the library and the world. It was, even if she was going to be modest about it, kind of a big deal.

Her brother and sister were staring at her. "Go away. I'm reading," she said.

And her shocked brother and sister backed away and left her alone.

That, surely, was true magic.

✳ How to Read to a Dragon ✳

Beneath every library in the world there sleeps a dragon. Whether or not you're a wizard, you can help give those dragons sweet and fascinating dreams by reading to them. If you're not very close to a library, you can practice reading out loud at home for your next visit. But if you don't like reading out loud, dragons can also listen to you reading in your mind.

So what kinds of books do dragons like best? It depends on the dragon, of course, but the best approach is to give them a varied diet. Here are some types of books you could read to a dragon.

- Books with facts, about spacecraft and inventions and forests and trains and animals and germs and cities and farms and dinosaurs. Dragons don't live in the waking world most of the time, and reading them fact books gives them a view into the human world that they wouldn't get otherwise.

- Books with wizards—it makes them feel comforted and at home.
- Books about dragons—everyone likes to read stories that are about themselves from time to time.
- Science fiction—dragons love to think about how the world could be and what the future will bring. Also, spaceships are awesome.
- Fairy tales and other traditional stories— old stories that get passed down by word of mouth are very powerful, because every person who tells them adds their own magic. Each old story can spawn a thousand new ones. Dragons like stories that are alive like that.
- Stories set in the past—this is called historical fiction. It's not the same as history, but it sends your imagination back into the past. Dragons live outside of time, so historical stories feel just as real and present to them as ones from

now. Time is a made-up, human thing.

- Books of maps—so many amazing stories start with a place. So many place-names lead to new stories. Dragons love maps.
- The next book in this series—*The Monster in the Lake*, about the further adventures of Kit and friends. That will definitely please your local dragon.

Happy reading!

✳ ACKNOWLEDGMENTS ✳

Some of you might not know how much you helped me write and publish this book. Surprise! There are more whom I will inevitably remember the second this goes to print.

- Karen, my wife, my first reader, my cocreator. This book would not exist without you, and my world would be a far less magical place.
- My parents, for giving me dragons, wizards, and libraries early in life.
- Polly, my agent. A guide, champion, and editor all in one.
- Tom, my editor, fellow frost fan, shaper of the library.
- Davide, who brought Kit's library so perfectly to life.
- Elisabetta, design maestro, champion of neon.
- The Nosy Crow team, for your expertise, enthusiasm, and trusting me not to steal your dog.
- The Girls. For your faces, always.
- Robin Stevens, for sneks and puppies.
- David Stevens. You know what you did.
- Mel, for all your cheerleading.

- Gus and Margot, who have so many stories ahead of them.
- Clan Roberts, who is morally obliged to buy my books.
- Mariam and all of Feminism 2.0, for making me think.
- The pocket friends, for snark and kindness.
- Buffy (the dog), without whom Dogon would not exist.
- *Buffy* (the show), without which I would have no wife, dog, or fascination with things lurking beneath libraries.
- Samantha, Virginie, Ammara, Mel (again), and Louisa D. Thank you for making my book better.
- Zoey D. and Matt F., for knowing libraries are portals to other worlds, and worlds in their own right.
- Milla, Alex S.B., Mason, Mac, Dan V., Rob Deb, Dave S., Rob W., Katherine S., Beatrice, Beth, and Onika: true originals and inspirations for so many years.
- Aisha and the newbies, for your bottomless support and support via pictures of bottoms.
- Laura, Chairman of Biznis.
- Chloe, for the DMs.

- Shannon; not a librarian, but who gets books to the children as a matter of urgency.
- Nikesh, for showing me there *are* more hours in the day.
- Lindsay, for the submission trenches.
- Stuart, for cats and space robots.
- Ming, for roti and sympathy.
- Sarwat and the Hatters, for cocktails and victories.
- Cathy, Albert, Jamie, and Kelly, for believing in me.
- Imogen, for walks in the park.
- Anne and Jim, for blissful writing retreats.
- Kirsty, Kay, Mark, Cori, Ravyn, Joey, Whitenight, Nikki, and all of Buffyworld that was. My imagination grew nine sizes there.
- Alice S.H., for reading the zombie novel that's in a drawer (for now).
- Emma D., now N., for being there while I wrote my very first book.
- Stoke Newington Bookshop, for stocking the best children's books and dog treats in north London.
- I'd also like to thank current political reality, for giving me something worth escaping from.

ABOUT THE AUTHOR & ILLUSTRATOR

LOUIE STOWELL started her career writing carefully researched books about space, ancient Egypt, politics, and science, but eventually she lapsed into just making stuff up. She likes writing about dragons, wizards, vampires, fairies, monsters, and parallel worlds. Louie Stowell lives in London with her wife, Karen; her dog, Buffy; and a creepy puppet that is probably cursed.

DAVIDE ORTU is an Italian artist who began his career in graphic design before discovering children's book illustration. He is on a quest to conjure colorful and fantastic places where time stops to offer the biggest emotions to the smallest people. Davide Ortu lives in Spain.